THE GIRL IN THE
POLKA-DOT DRESS

THE GIRL IN THE POLKA-DOT DRESS

Beryl Bainbridge

WINDSOR
PARAGON

First published 2011
by Little, Brown
This Large Print edition published 2011
by AudioGO Ltd
by arrangement with Little, Brown Book Group

Hardcover ISBN: 978 1 445 85898 2
Softcover   ISBN: 978 1 445 85899 9

British Library Cataloguing in Publication Data available

Printed and bound in Great Britain by
MPG Books Group Limited

CHAPTER ONE

Earlier that morning, on the eighteenth of May, Washington Harold had fled abreast of a mob hurling cans, sticks and stones at the windows lining the boulevard. It wasn't personal, simply a matter of being in the wrong place at the wrong time; he shouldn't have stalked Artie Brune's cat.

Now, at three thirty in the afternoon, he was sitting inside the cabin of his newly bought secondhand camper, waiting for Wheeler's woman from England. Not a speck of dirt on the dashboard, every last streak removed with a square of cloth, clean even behind the miniature clock with the face of Abe Lincoln stamped beneath the numerals. Pity about the rain throwing up squirts of mud against the paintwork; protected by the coat of polish given before the weather turned bad, it should wipe off. Wheeler's girl would be knocked out by the whole thing—the icebox, the basin with the running water, the little snazzy curtains. They'd get to know each other real well and sunset time, wearing her polka-dot dress, she would toss the salad while he fixed drinks and made the fire; later, dark time, he'd stab his fingers at the heavens and list the names of the stars.

If they really hit it off he might even take her into his confidence as regards Wheeler. Not everything of course. From what he remembered of her, he doubted if she would understand much of what he intended. Though not unintelligent she was far from educated. Some things, ordinary things like the workings of Wall Street and the aims of political

1

groups, were foreign to her, which made it all the more puzzling that Wheeler had become attached to her. But then, Wheeler was a womaniser, while he, Harold Grasse, was considered shy. A shy kid and an unapproachable adult. Not exactly that, more that he was cautious, choosy.

He leaned back and tried to fit all of his face into the oval mirror but saw only his forehead, balding and still tanned from an earlier vacation in Florida. A touch of the Willie Shakespeares about that brow, domed, intellectual, though it had to be admitted his grades at college hadn't been great.

He peered through the wash of rain that obliterated the airport buildings and the concrete rectangle of parking lot. Deeper into Maryland and the weather would be just fine. He'd put on his shorts and maybe her hand would sink onto his leg, and she'd stroke the skin with her fingers. Judging by the tone of their correspondence, she was a hell of a friendly girl, if somewhat hysterical. That time he'd walked her home in England, she'd gripped his hand on the excuse that the street was dangerous. Death under the streetlamps, she intimated, could strike at any time.

Smoothing out the crumpled paper on his lap he read again the letter from the woman he was waiting to meet.

Harold dear,
All in a rush and feeling maybe I should not
be doing this. People have been so nice, you
have no idea. My friend in the room below has
lent me a pair of slacks and Polly two jumpers
and a skirt. Arn't people kind? Also I cashed in
my dividends due from the Co-op, £6 and 15

2

*shillings in all, which has let me buy some sun
oil and a new dress with polka-dots all over. The
frock is an extravagance but not the oil as my
skin is very sensitive due to my mother suffering
from pernicious anemia before I was born and
having been subjected to gold treatment, an old
fashioned medicine now considered dangerous.
A district nurse came every day and injected
her with a kind of hypodermic reserved for sick
horses. About money—I have only managed
to gather together about the equivilent of 47
dollars. I thought I better tell you this in advance
as I am so embaressed at the meagerness of
my contribution when compared with your
generosity. Polly would have given me money,
but I didn't like to ask. As our letters will cross
I wonder if you have heard anything yet of the
whereabouts of Dr Wheeler. The whole business
is very exciting and I can't help thinking that fate
has drawn us together. Dr Wheeler may be dead
. . . I'm prepared for that. I read somewhere that
life should be regarded as a dream, and death as
an awakening, though I don't really know what
that means, unless it's religious. Enough . . .
kisses . . . Rose.*

*p.s. I don't doubt that when we catch up with
Dr Wheeler he will reburse you for what I have
recieved.*
p.p.s. Scuse spelling.

It was useful, he thought, that she appeared to be
labouring under an obligation. It would make her
more compliant when the time came.

Rose hadn't liked the sound the aircraft made as it tore through the sky, and it must have made her breathe heavily because the man in the next seat kept urging her to relax and take hold of his hand. All her life people had been telling her what to do, even strangers, which was curious. He was quite a nice man, in spite of him confiding that his wife had bad breath, so she did as he suggested. It didn't help.

It was a mistake to refuse the umbrella offered at the door of the plane. She ran with bent head towards the arrival building and entered with hair flattened and stockings splattered. Waiting damply for her suitcase to be cleared, she strained to glimpse Washington Harold through the glass doors. Where was the constant sunshine, the brightness of high summer?

The arrival lounge was half empty and she picked him out at once, leaning against a wall with his hands in his pockets. His beard, though he had written of it, was a surprise. The colour of dying daffodils, it was thick and wide, as though he was a sea captain.

He said, 'Well, I guess you made it.'

She said, 'Yes . . . isn't this rain dreadful.'

'It's been bad for some days,' he assured her, leading the way through the doors into the deluge.

She saw nothing save a grey landscape blotted with cars and swept by water. He halted and pointed with obvious pleasure at a large vehicle at the edge of the parking lot.

'Isn't she something,' he crowed.

She said, 'Oh, yes . . . lovely.' Water was running

down her face now and seeping beneath the collar of her coat. She stood on one leg and clenched her teeth to stop them from chattering.

'You cold, Rose?'

'Not really. I'm tired, I think . . . after the flight. The time thing, I expect.'

She was relieved that he'd used her name. It made her feel less of a stranger. All the same, she was embarrassed at the meeting and suddenly appalled at arriving.

At last he was opening the doors of the van and shoving her case inside. She could see cupboards and a sort of cooker, and what appeared to be a rolled-up mattress. 'It's very nice,' she said.

Opening the side door, he warned that the step was high up, but he didn't offer a helping hand when she hauled herself into the passenger seat. The woodwork was yellow, highly polished, the seats covered in plastic. She watched his blurred figure move past the window and wished she was back home in Kentish Town. Once inside, he made no effort to start the engine, just sat there holding the shiny wheel.

'It's a lovely van,' she enthused, thinking he needed encouragement. 'It must have cost a fortune.'

'It's not a van,' he corrected, 'it's a camper. There's an icebox, hanging space for clothes, a folding table, and the seating comes down to make a bed. Know what I mean?'

She was thinking what he really meant was that they weren't going to spend nights in boarding houses as she'd supposed. Surely he didn't expect her to lie beside him? They'd been writing to each other for over a year, planning the details, but there had never been the slightest hint, not the slightest suggestion . . .

'The only thing missing,' he said, 'is a luggage rack for the roof. I thought we might go look for one on our way back to the apartment. That all right with you?'

'Of course,' she said. 'I'm all yours.' He started the engine and drove out of the airport, the great rubber tyres throwing up spray.

She looked out of the window to see something strange in her surroundings, something to prove home was far away. There was little out there save other cars, bigger than usual but not really so different, not if you went to the pictures a lot. She thought Harold must be loaded with money, bothering about a luggage rack when there was all that space behind. 'So many cars,' she murmured.

'Oldsmobile, Chevrolet, Ford, Lincoln, Mustang, Plymouth, Dodge,' he recited, as though remembering a poem.

'The plane was marvellous,' she gushed. 'So much food they give you . . . all that drink. A gentleman who spoke candidly of his wife treated me to champagne . . . wasn't that kind of him? He'd been away on business, first in Tokyo, then in Ireland.' Only the bit about the business trips was true; she hadn't been bought champagne.

Harold mumbled a reply, something about the rain. He drove with one hand, the other tugging at his beard.

'I'm sorry you had to send all those particulars to the American Embassy,' she said.

'Say, what gave there? What was the idea?' He was giving her his attention now.

'When I applied for the visa I had to say how

6

much moncy I was taking with me. And the reason for the visit. I couldn't really explain that. I mean, I couldn't say I was looking for Dr Wheeler when I didn't really know where he was.'

She stopped, worried that he might take that the wrong way. She hadn't meant it as a criticism, just that the Embassy had gone on about her possibly becoming a public charge or whatever. She'd had to declare that she was only taking fourteen pounds with her. Bernard said they simply wanted to make sure they weren't going to have to fork out for the flight home. Polly said they were within their rights to make enquiries, and that it was odd of Harold not to enclose a return ticket. As a seasoned traveller he should have been aware of the rules.

She said, 'When we find Dr Wheeler, he'll pay you back . . . I know he will.' Harold didn't reply, just kept pulling at his captain's beard. Perhaps he was so rich he wasn't bothered.

They drove down an avenue of cars for sale, neon advertisements cutting gold dollars through the wet sky. 'This stretch,' he said, 'fully illustrates a free society enjoying the privileges of free enterprise.'

She said, 'I see,' though she didn't.

'Just look at that goddamned monstrosity,' he shouted, pointing a finger at a Disney castle bright lemon in colour and festooned with fairy lights. 'Have you ever seen anything like it?'

'We've got Blackpool,' she said. He sounded quite fanatical.

They turned left into another grey square and drove towards a concrete building with glass panels. There was a flag dripping from a pole in the middle of the parking lot.

'Sears Roebuck,' Harold announced. 'Greatest store in the world . . . for quantity, not quality. Everything from a pair of socks to a Buick. Take your pick.'

She would have preferred to stay where she was and straighten her stockings, but he had jumped out and was waiting for her to follow. Already his brown suede boots were darkening under the rain. Bedraggled, she trailed behind him into the store, shoes slapping over the tiles, eyes glittery from the glare of lights splashing across chrome and steel.

He drew her attention to the clocks with illuminated dials, and asked, 'Do you have this sort of thing in England?'

'I expect we do. I don't really know about cars.'

'The automobile industry,' he said, 'is catering more and more for women. It's who they aim for now.' His tone was contemptuous.

Everything was available, mirrors to go on the dashboard, heaters, tartan rugs, mountains of scatter cushions covered in plastic, mottled to resemble animal hide, lines of mascots with dangling limbs and eyes that turned jungle red as they spun.

'Didn't Wheeler own a car?' Harold asked.

'I don't think so. He was always on foot when we met.'

'Doesn't sound like the Wheeler I knew. He was strictly an automobile man.'

He seemed undecided what to do. There were several salesmen hovering about, yet he just stood there, shoulders bowed.

She had to sit down. That morning she had worked four hours behind the reception desk at Mr McCready's dental practice in Cavendish Square, travelled on a coach to Heathrow, spent countless hours shuddering though the heavens, only to find that time had stood still and the day had scarcely moved on.

Harold ambled away and studied fire extinguishers. She hadn't remembered he had a stoop and bleached eyelashes. Polly had met him at some conference to do with the lasting damage done to children whose mothers had been deserted by their spouses. She'd said he was remarkably prejudiced against fleeing fathers—for an American, that is. Rose had nodded approval, out of politeness. To her way of thinking, absent dads were something to be encouraged.

There were no seats as such, so she perched herself on an upright heater and was confronted by a pyramid of lit headlamps under bulging glass; it was like being in an operating theatre. Out of the walls came the sound of a piano, notes pattering upon the silver machinery. She closed her eyes, and Dr Wheeler came through the darkness, the brim of his trilby hat rocking in the sea breeze.

They sat on separate tombstones for a while, not speaking, listening to the wind soughing through the pine trees. He wore a blue muffler tucked into the top of his duffle coat and knitted gloves. Once he leaned forward and shoved her hand away from her mouth, woolly fingers scratchy against her chin. Then he began to lecture her on Napoleon, in particular about the French soldiers who had perished trying to conquer Russia. She said it must be awful to be responsible for thousands of deaths, and he said numbers didn't matter, that to be the cause of even one death was reprehensible. He didn't look at her, but then he never did, not directly, not eye to eye.

9

Perhaps, she countered, Napoleon had been bullied as a child . . . by his father. He remained silent, staring upwards at the clouds scudding above the swaying trees.

Someone was shaking her shoulder, thrusting her backwards and forwards. 'You passing out on me?' Harold demanded.

'Please don't,' she protested, 'I'm very tired,' and slumped there, sagging under his hand.

He didn't express sympathy, just pulled her upright.

'I'm sorry to be such a nuisance.' She could hear the whine in her voice. 'Did you find the roof rack?'

'Sure, sure. If it fits, it will do fine.'

He took a long time to procure the right attachments, even longer to write out the cheque. Then there was food to be bought, oil, salad, a Jewish loaf, slabs of red meat. Outside it was still raining.

It was over an hour before they reached his apartment. Once they had left the freeway and entered a neighbourhood of redbrick houses bordered by tattered plane trees it might have been London, except for the mailboxes on stilts and the length of the cars. At a crossing near a furniture store they were halted by three men in yellow oilskins diverting the traffic. Ahead, black smoke curled into the sky.

Harold swore and reversed into a side street. He said there was a disturbance downtown. Following the assassination of Martin Luther King Jr, there were riots all over the States. Being so close to Washington, Baltimore was particularly affected. 'The negroes aren't putting up with it any more,' he said. 'They've had enough.'

10

'Where I was born,' Rosc told him, 'there were lots of coloured people. We never really noticed them.'

She was taken aback by Harold's apartment. Having only films to go on, she was not prepared for the drabness of his sitting room. It had a naked bulb hanging from the high ceiling and a sofa draped in a yellow blanket. Above the electric fire, propped on a shelf, was a dull picture of a house on a hill. The wall behind the cooker was spattered with fat.

'It's very cosy,' she said.

'Not a word I'd use,' he said.

She wanted to lie down, anywhere, preferably on the floor. The sofa she sat on had something harsh thrusting through the blanket. 'Please,' she begged, 'I must rest,' but he insisted she should eat something first. She didn't know him well enough to argue.

It took him time to grill the meat. When he peeled the onions he mopped his watery eyes with his fingers, and then wiped them on the front of his trousers. Everything he did was slow and measured, as though he was sleepwalking. She had to keep talking because he hardly ever spoke, and how could she remain silent in this stranger's room, a stranger who had paid out so much money to bring her here? She asked him questions—how long had he lived in this house, how much did the flat cost? In the circumstances, it was absurd she knew so little about his life.

Usually, with a few words, she provoked conversation, but not this time. The only thing that aroused a response was when she wanted to know if he'd always travelled a lot. That's when he told

11

her he'd gone to Chicago a month past to look for Dr Wheeler. He hadn't found him, of course, because her letter informing him that Wheeler had moved to Washington had arrived too late.

Again she apologised, squirming on the uncomfortable sofa.

'You needing the bathroom?' Harold asked. 'It's through there.'

When she stood, she noticed him look at her legs, quickly and away again, not boldly.

The bathroom was tiled and none too clean. There was a torn curtain of plastic slung sideways from the bath. The tub, similar to the one she used in Kentish Town, stood on cast-iron legs, old and rusted. Judging from the state of the toilet bowl, Americans didn't know about Vim. Which was funny seeing the way Harold, the evening she had invited him in for a coffee, had rubbed his finger across her bedside table and commented on the grime.

He'd been staying with her friends Polly and Bernard, and she'd been asked round for dinner to make a foursome. She hadn't really wanted to go because of the name Grasse, which she reckoned sounded German. While she was still at school her class had been marched in crocodile to the Philharmonic Hall to watch a film to do with British soldiers tidying up a concentration camp. There were bulldozers raking up funny scarecrows and tipping them into pits. Later, Mavis, the head prefect, said they were dead bodies. Nobody could possibly be friendly with a Jerry, not when one knew what had happened to the Jews. But then Polly told her Washington Harold was himself Jewish, so that made it all right.

12

After the meal, it was suggested that Harold should escort her home; the road past the bread factory was dark and sometimes drunks fell down in the gutter.

Rose knew about men. She'd been on her own, off and on, in London since she was sixteen, and had often found herself in difficult situations. It was due to politeness, mostly. Mother had instilled in her that if you really wanted something, like a second piece of cake, you had to say no. And if the cake was awful and you didn't want another piece, you said yes, so as not to offend. Once, a man had bought her drinks in a pub in South Kensington and then taken her to his room near the Brompton Oratory. It was a posh area, so she didn't think anything could go wrong. After all, it was only the dispossessed who needed to exert power. The man had forced her onto his bed, knocking a tooth out in his struggle to hold her down. Bloody-mouthed, she said she'd do whatever he wanted if he'd just let her use the toilet first. As she fled down the stairs he'd emptied a cup of water over the landing banisters, and she'd fancied he was weeing on her. She'd gone to the police, but as she was under age they wanted the address of her parents. There was no way she was going to let Father know what had happened.

Which was why it was all right to invite Harold into her bedsitter. She'd known he wasn't the kind of man who needed to make an impression, at least not of that sort. Besides, he was a psychologist. That first evening, she'd even thought he hadn't noticed her—apart from her being in the same room as Bernard and Polly—until he asked her about Dr Wheeler's photograph on her bedside

13

table, that is. It wasn't a very good photo and had been taken eight years before, the time Dr Wheeler had come up to London to say his goodbyes before leaving England for good. It was her nineteenth birthday and he'd given her an old Brownie camera that he said had belonged to his sister. She'd snapped him standing outside Charing Cross station, capturing his image a second before he raised a hand to blot out his face. He was wearing his trilby hat.

Washington Harold hadn't told her he recognised Dr Wheeler, simply stood there holding the framed picture to his chest as though accepting a bunch of flowers.

The meal was ready when Rose returned to the kitchen. There wasn't a tablecloth.

She said, 'That place where you bought the roof rack for the van—'

'Camper,' he corrected.

'I thought I was in the cottage hospital having my appendix out.'

'Odd,' he said, but she could tell he wasn't listening.

While they ate he told her his plans for the following day. They would pack first thing and then go into town to see his broker; then they'd head off for Washington.

'Gosh,' she said, wolfing down the bubbling meat.

He kept filling her glass with red wine and she drank it to make the time pass quicker. After a while she felt much better, was even confident enough to light a cigarette without asking permission. When she leaned back to blow out smoke he looked at her chest. She smiled and felt

14

on top of things. Presently he said there were a lot of last-minute jobs that needed doing, but as she was obviously in no condition to be of assistance she better get to her bed. Though this was possibly a rebuke, she continued to smile. The bedroom, he told her, was the second door down the hall.

She didn't bother to clean her teeth, even though the brush was brand new. Changed into her nightgown, she stared at her surroundings. The room was devoid of pictures, of ornaments. There was a newspaper picture of a woman pinned to the back of the door, but she was too hazy in the head to read the caption. A vent in the skirting board blew out hot air; the pile of the carpet swam like dust across her toes. Peering through the shutters she saw a veranda with a rocking chair, the backs of some tenement houses, rubbish bins in rows, a great plane tree dripping water, and a black cat circling round and round the van; Harold was kneeling on its roof, the sky turning dark blue behind his head.

There was a smell about the bed, a staleness. The sheets were clean but there was an odour of long ago dampness. She knew that smell. Years ago, suffering from toothache, she had got into Father's bed for warmth. Normally she slept with Mother in the room with the statue of Adam and Eve on the windowsill, only the pain had made her whinge a lot and Mother had banished her onto the landing. She remembered the occasion, not on account of the toothache but because Father had been wearing nothing but a string vest, and when he turned in his sleep his thingie lolled against her leg. It stung, like a bee.

She fell asleep with her hand cupped over her nose and woke with Harold lying alongside. 'You,'

15

she exclaimed, as though it ought to be someone else.

'I've fixed the luggage rack,' he said, as if that explained the proximity.

She sat upright and asked what time it was. He said, 'Three o'clock, Rose.'

'Night or day?' she enquired, which made him laugh.

He pulled her down, telling her she must have a good rest for the journey ahead. He didn't attempt to put an arm round her, nor did he lie too close. She heard him scratching his beard as she sank again into sleep.

CHAPTER TWO

Harold woke to pale skies and nicked his forefinger when slicing bread for toast. Dwelling on the day before, he congratulated himself on the way things had gone. Rose had obviously enjoyed the visit to Sears Roebuck and been impressed by his apartment, unremarkable though it was. When he recalled the squalor of her Victorian bedsitter in London, this was hardly surprising. True, she hadn't been of much help when it came to packing, but then she probably felt shy of handling his personal belongings, boxer shorts and such like.

Remembering she hadn't washed before going to bed—he'd been obliged to sleep with his head well above the covers—he ran a bath and attempted to rouse her. Her response was unexpected; she punched out at him and snuggled deeper under the covers. Reminded of Dollie, he left the room. Toast

16

eaten and too agitated to fry his usual breakfast eggs, he busied himself stacking suitcases into the camper: the extra blankets, tinned foods and cans of gasoline he stored on the luggage rack, along with a leather case full of documents. Throughout his comings and goings Rose remained dead to the world, save for an audible wheeze to her breathing. He was on hands and knees inside the camper when his neighbour, Artie Brune, poked his head through the doors.

'I guess she come,' Artie said, eyes spiteful.

Harold nodded.

'She up for it?'

'You bet,' he enthused, and would have turned his back if he hadn't thought Brune might later have reason to remember his attitude.

Artie complained that his Ma wasn't feeling too good. 'She been taken to the hospital,' he said.

'That's too bad,' Harold murmured.

Artie wasn't sure how sick she was. She'd been a bad mother but if she was dying he should stick around, shouldn't he?

Harold said he should.

'When she humping men, she tell me sleep out on fire steps. Once in snow. That ain't good, is it?'

'No, it isn't,' Harold said. In his head he was going over what he would do when they got to Washington. Rose would have to go into the Stanfords' apartment on her own. By way of excuse he'd tell her it wasn't safe to leave the camper unattended, not with the disturbances still going on; after all, it was no more than the truth.

An hour later, when he returned indoors, he caught Rose about to open a cardboard box he'd left on the table. He pushed her aside and, snatching it up, ran from the room. Stuffing it inside the pillowcase he'd prepared, he stowed it on the roof beneath the army blankets. When he'd fixed the tarpaulin in place he went back inside to make his peace with Rose. He reckoned she would be feeling pretty awkward, possibly tearful. He told her he was sorry for his roughness and meant it.

She said, 'Don't mention it. I should have remembered that curiosity killed the cat.'

He was thrown by her tone of voice, the defiant way she met his gaze, and heard himself giving reasons for his behaviour. 'At night,' he said, 'when we make camp, there could be snakes, certainly poisonous insects . . . not to mention flies. We need powerful repellents.'

'I don't mind flies,' she said. 'All through my childhood we had sticky paper hanging from the light bulb.'

Flustered, he told her they were almost ready to leave. When he knew her better he might confide that he preferred snakes to flies.

He went into the bathroom to check he'd packed his tablets, and saw her toothbrush still in its wrapper. Taking it through, he was about to ask if she intended to use it, but stopped himself. It wouldn't do to boss her around, not until he'd gained her confidence. All the same, it was important to keep her in her place. He said, mildly, 'You were pretty out of it this morning. I'd run you a bath.'

'I don't need a bath. I had one before I left London.'

'You swore at me. If I hadn't stepped back you might have busted my nose.'

'I thought you were my dad. He was always

18

shaking me awake to get me off to school.'

'I just wanted to give you time to get ready,' he said. 'We should get going. I've business to do at the bank, and with my broker.'

She was smiling at him now, face flushed with anticipation, eager to know how many days it would take them to get to Washington.

'Not days,' he said. 'It's a matter of hours . . . two or three at the most. It depends on how bad the disturbances were last night.'

Bewildered, she asked him why they needed the van if they were so near.

'Because,' he said, 'I doubt if Wheeler will still be at the address he gave you. I reckon he's on the move.'

Looking at her he was surprised at the sudden shadow of fear in her eyes. The pink had fled her cheeks. It occurred to him that she was not as bold as she liked to pretend and he felt protective; fear was something he understood.

He didn't tell her that he had got hold of a forwarding address for Wheeler when visiting Chicago, nor that the Stanfords, occupants of the apartment outside Washington, were in possession of a letter which they refused to hand over to him, insisting they'd been told it should only be given to the girl from England. He would have offered them money but they weren't that sort of folk.

He asked Rose if she was ready to leave. She was wearing slacks and a creased blouse under a raincoat; she hadn't brushed her hair. Perhaps he should have told her they were having dinner that night with the Shaefers.

Artie Brune was lounging against the hood of the camper when they went outside. 'I heard a lot

19

about you, girl,' he said, looking Rose up and down. It was obvious from the twist of his mouth that she was not the beddable woman he'd pictured.

Rose climbed into the front seat and stared straight ahead. When Harold started the engine, she asked, 'That man, is he a friend of yours?'

'Yes,' he said, though it was an exaggeration; only Artie's cat came under that heading.

She didn't utter another word as they drove into central Baltimore. He kept up a commentary of where they were, but when he glanced sideways she was looking down at her lap, twisting her top lip between her fingers, ignoring the gangs of workmen boarding up store windows and raking glass into the gutters. On 26th Street the doors to the synagogue had been blooded with red paint.

'Dear God,' he exclaimed, nudging her with his elbow. Her head jerked up, but still she remained silent. He couldn't tell whether she was sulking or merely tired. He had to slow down as they approached Wild Bill's Firearms store, on account of the number of police patrolling the sidewalk.

He parked beyond the Medical Library and told her he would be as quick as he could. A fire was still burning at the lower end of St Paul's Street and he was obliged to make a detour. He left a letter at the bank, to be opened in the event of his death, and a copy with his broker. He took pride in keeping his life orderly.

On his return he found Rose gone from the camper; she'd left her shoes behind. He strode up and down, and just as alarm was spiralling into anger spied her sauntering barefoot along the opposite sidewalk. 'The camper,' he bawled, 'it isn't locked.' She waved at him, dismissively, and

20

shouted back, 'No need to get het up . . . I kept an eye open.' He climbed into the driving seat and forced himself to remain calm.

She took her time crossing the street and settling in beside him. She said, 'It's funny, isn't it? A shop selling guns, like as if they were carrots and turnips.'

He couldn't reply, not civilly.

'When I was little,' she burbled, 'I wanted a toy gun more than anything, but they weren't making them because of the war. So I sawed Mother's yard brush in two and tied a piece of elastic from one end to the other, with a cork at the top. It didn't work very well but it was better than nothing. I ran around shooting Germans. Mother was cross . . . on account of her broom.'

'I'll bet,' he ground out.

'Then one day I was playing in the back field when an enemy plane passed overhead. It had got lost from a previous raid or something. It came down so low I could see the airman. He started firing his machine gun . . .'

A memory of Carl Bloomfield came into his mind, a second-year freshman who swore that his father had been so addicted to the camera that he had paused to take a photograph when Bloomfield had gone under in a swimming pool, and again when he had smashed into a wall when learning to drive.

Rose said, 'My mother was in a window at the back of our house. She was screaming.'

Only Shaefer had thought Bloomfield something other than a fantasist. He held that the expression in Bloomfield's eyes nudged the truth.

'I hid in the bushes,' Rose said, 'and heard the

21

bullets slashing the grass.'

Nobody had believed Shaefer, not until Bloomfield went home for Thanksgiving and gunned down his parents while the turkey was being carved.

'No wonder Mr Kennedy got killed,' Rose said. 'Or that Luther King.'

'Tonight,' Harold told her, 'we're having dinner with a man who was in the same hotel as Dr King the day he was shot.'

'Crikey.'

He asked her if she was hungry; his own belly was growling. She said she didn't care for food. 'We all eat far too much,' she told him. 'It destroys the brain.' She sat slumped beside him, bare feet propped on the dashboard, toenails rimmed with dirt. She was sucking her thumb.

She was not an easy companion, that was for sure. He switched on the radio to subdue the silence. Someone was rasping out a jazz song . . . *Here's a photo of me when I was three . . . And here's my pony too. Here's a picnic we had. And Jane with dad . . . Here's me in love with you.* Embarrassed by the sentiments he reached forward to turn the dial.

'Leave it,' she cried, 'it's so lovely,' and shoved his hand away with her foot.

He wondered if it had crossed Bloomfield's mind to take a snapshot of his mother and father sprawled across the Thanksgiving table.

'The word photography,' he said, 'is from the Greek. It means drawing from light.'

Rose didn't respond.

Here's our house in Maine . . . and me again . . . that's me in love with you, wailed the voice.

Two blocks before they came to the freeway the

22

camper was brought to a halt. An elderly woman, black fists punching the air, was being manhandled into a patrol car. He wound up the window to drown the screams spilling from her mouth.

It took over three hours to reach the outskirts of Washington. Having gone without his breakfast eggs he needed food. Stopping at a roadside diner near Gaithersburg he'd asked Rose to come with him, but she refused.

When he got back behind the wheel he could tell she'd been smoking; he didn't open the window because he liked the smell of tobacco.

Most of the time Rose appeared to doze, until they passed the sign for Bethesda and she sat up and quite animatedly remarked that it was a name she remembered from scripture lessons at school. It intrigued him how often she mentioned things from her childhood. It struck him they were alike; the past had eclipsed the present.

A sloping path bordered with cherry trees led up to the front porch of the Stanfords' detached house. Rose didn't immediately get out; she was fidgeting with her lip again.

He said, 'There was a famous architect called Stanford. He designed Madison Square Garden . . . in New York. He was murdered.'

'By his wife?' she murmured.

'No,' he retorted. 'He was a womaniser, shot by an outraged husband. Women don't kill.'

Still she didn't move. At last, opening the camper door, she surprised him by asking if he was coming with her.

'Best not,' he said. 'It's right you see him on your own . . . at first.'

Watching her go up the path, shoulders hunched

against the rain, he felt guilty at not telling her the truth. As soon as he saw her enter the house he drove further down the street.

Everything about Rose puzzled him: her manners, her background, most of all her link with Wheeler. Seeing that blurred photograph on her dusty bedside table had shaken him. Her story about meeting him in some remote coastal village in the north of England sixteen years ago simply didn't make sense. What was he doing holed up in the back of beyond? Rose had no idea what sort of work he'd been doing; she'd never asked, she said, because she'd been taught it was rude to enquire what people did for a living.

He'd consulted Jesse Shaefer who'd reluctantly hinted in a roundabout way that Wheeler's stay in England might have had something to do with the Jupiter missiles stationed in Turkey; he refused to elaborate further. Shaefer's explanation was possibly near to the truth. Rose said Wheeler had frequently been absent—on holiday she thought— because he was sunburnt when everyone else was pale.

His own first encounter with Wheeler had taken place seven years before, through Shaefer. It was at a reception to mark the appointment of the President's brother as Attorney General. Wheeler wore a grey suit and classy brown shoes. When he crossed a room he glided rather than walked, head slightly inclined. Sometimes, when speaking, he shielded his eyes with his hand, the way people did when gazing into the distance. It wasn't altogether contrived, simply that he was one of those fortunate people who made an impression. He was aware of it, for sure, but then who could blame him?

24

Recognition was something everyone craved, if only to prove they existed. During the following twelve months they had dined together on half a dozen occasions, Wheeler always picking up the cheque; at the climax of the year, complimentary tickets had arrived for the game between the Green Bay Packers and the New York Giants. Wheeler hadn't turned up, but afterwards a bunch of red roses with a card expressing apologies had been delivered to Dollie.

It had been flattering to be sought after by such an important man, one at the centre of things, at least until the real motives for his interest had been exposed. Which was why it was hard to understand his involvement with Rose. When he'd first met her it couldn't have been sexual. She was only a child and he wasn't a fool. Nor, judging from the way Rose described their last meeting in London, the visit to Madame Tussaud's to drool over the Battle of Waterloo, that last cup of coffee in the station refreshment bar, had it ever developed into anything more intimate. And yet it was apparent they had been close, because some of the sentiments she expressed were too heavy with perverse meaning to have stemmed from a mind as uninformed as her own. The night before, chin greasy from her steak, fork stabbing in the direction of his breast, she had declared that soon they would all grow old, that in empty rooms they would dream of those who had slammed a door too long ago to be of importance.

Rose returned an hour later; she didn't seem too upset at not finding Wheeler. Mrs Stanford, she reported, had rugs on the wall and a picture of Walt Whitman in the lavatory. She'd been given a cup of tea without milk.

'No sign of Wheeler?' he asked.

'You were right,' she said. 'He left some time ago. A man came round a few weeks back looking for him, but he wouldn't give his name.'

He said, 'I guess Wheeler knew lots of people.'

She took an envelope out of her pocket. It had her name typed on the front. She said, 'They were jolly informative about who might be the next president. There's Richard Nixon, Hubert Humphrey, Eugene McCarthy, Robert Kennedy, Jimmy Wallace—'

'George,' he corrected.

'Whoever,' she said, crumpling the letter in her fist. He looked sideways at her and saw a tear splash from her cheek.

CHAPTER THREE

The Shaefers lived on the seventh floor of a converted warehouse off Connecticut Avenue. Harold maintained it was a very exclusive neighbourhood, which was why there was nobody on foot in the streets. If you went anywhere you got into an automobile.

Mrs Shaefer opened the door to them. She was short and stout and wore a stained apron over a long black dress. Before she said hallo she swore at a man with a ponytail who was standing behind her. She called him a shithead. Rose felt at home. The man with the hair tied back gave Harold a bear hug.

Mrs Shaefer took Rose into a bedroom and told her to throw her raincoat onto the bed. Rose protested it was wet. Mrs Shaefer said she couldn't care less. 'What time did you get here?' she asked. 'Have you seen anything of the city?'

Rose said that Harold had made her get out of the van to stand at the railings outside the grounds of the White House. He'd explained it was in the Colonial style. She'd liked the magnolia trees. Then he'd taken her to see the Executive Buildings.

'He told me,' she said, 'that Mr Truman thought them inefficient and wanted them pulled down but Mr Kennedy wouldn't let him.'

'Trust Harold,' said Mrs Shaefer. 'Always the man for exciting information.'

Drinks were served in a room as large as a hotel lounge. It had three leather settees and green glass doors opening onto a balcony. Rose was given a tall glass of something that looked like lemonade. It tasted fizzy and was colourless save for a piece of lemon that kept getting in the way. There were four other guests, a woman, a boy and two men, Bud and Bob. The woman was called Thora and wore white Bermuda shorts. Mrs Shaefer was addressed as George, her husband as Jesse. The boy didn't speak to anyone and left before the meal was served. Washington Harold had gone to the same school as all three men and on to university with Shaefer, who was a professor of constitutional law and was apparently often summoned to the President's office. No one explained why. There was a lot of talk about basketball and a coach named Curtis Parker.

Mr Shaefer seemed very angry with Lyndon Johnson. He said the man was insane, had turned the American Dream into the American Nightmare. Four days before announcing he

27

wouldn't accept nomination for a further term, he'd been thinking of invading Laos and sending another 200,000 soldiers to Vietnam.

'Mad as hell,' agreed Harold.

The woman in shorts confessed she'd once had terrible sexual problems with men. 'But then Daddy got me an analyst,' she confided, 'and now I'm all right.' Everybody spoke very loudly so as to be heard above the screech of cars in the street below.

Rose couldn't take anything in. The journey that morning had been a confusion of flyovers, underpasses, intersections, junctions, toll gates. Yield, the signs instructed in bright yellow. Sometimes there were fields full of cows, once a river, brown and swollen, once a town with a railway track running down the middle of its street. On either side, bursting back from the highway, the trees tossed rainwater. Nothing had stayed fixed in her head. She was an empty box, only dust under the lid. Not finding Dr Wheeler had upset her, though it had not come as a surprise. Deep down she'd known he wouldn't be there.

'Is it wise to go to Wanakena?' asked Mrs Shaefer; she was talking to Harold. It was the name of the place Dr Wheeler had given as a forwarding address.

'I guess not,' he replied. 'But what else can I do?'

'A phone call,' she suggested, but he shook his head. Rose thought he sounded different among friends, less censorious.

They sat down to dinner in a room circled with bookshelves; an owl in a glass case stood on a stool beside a radiator. There was a cup next to it with a fountain pen sticking out. Rose told Mrs Shaefer that high temperatures weren't good for stuffed

28

animals. She knew that because Father had told her about his sister Margaret falling into a depression after her pet, preserved in a pouncing position outside the door of the hot-water cupboard, had fallen apart from an infestation of moth.

'It was a tabby cat,' she said, 'called Nigger.'

Harold frowned. Mrs Shaefer smiled; her face, with its dark eyes, white skin and plump lips, appeared luminous.

Rose devoured everything on her plate, even the mess of salad leaves. Earlier, when Harold had decided to eat, she hadn't dared go with him for fear of diminishing her supply of money. She needed what little she had in case of an emergency, like running out of cigarettes. She'd smoked two while he was inside the café. He hadn't said he disliked smoking but she could tell he did by the peevish way he'd fluttered his fingers in the air when he got back into the van.

'You want more food?' asked Mrs Shaefer.

'Yes please, Jesse,' said Rose.

'George,' corrected Mrs Shaefer.

Rose said, 'Thank you so much. You're very kind.'

'My, you're polite,' said Thora.

There wasn't a pudding, just more drink and the lighting of cigarettes. Rose felt confident enough to scoop out her hunk of lemon. Mr Shaefer embarked on a discussion with Bud or Bob to do with the race problem. It grew very heated and at one point Mrs Shaefer got so irate she cuffed her husband over the head. He was going on about how misguided the new reforms would prove to be. It was right in one way, he argued, to give blacks equality, but in the end it wouldn't work.

29

The educated blacks would climb up, become as successful as whites, but the majority, the under-privileged, reliant on welfare and deprived of the incentive to survive, would forget the few honest ways they'd learned to earn a living and turn to crime. 'You think we have a problem now,' he shouted, 'just wait another thirty years. Remember Dollie's assessment of the future.' That's when Mrs Shaefer gave him a clout.

For a moment no one spoke. Rose sensed the sudden hush had nothing to do with black people. Then Washington Harold wiped his mouth with his hand and said, looking from her to Jesse Shaefer, 'She's interested in Martin Luther King Jr. I told her you were there.'

'I am,' Rose asserted. 'I really am. I went to a friend's house to watch him on the television.' She was telling the truth. She had watched the televised footage with Polly and Bernard. For some reason Polly had wept.

Jesse Shaefer embarked on a description of the events leading up to the assassination. Dr King had gone to Memphis in support of a march organised by people wanting the advancement of coloured persons. Poorly organised, it had turned into a riot. The police opened fire; result—one man dead, sixty injured. A committed pacifist, Dr King had quit Memphis.

Mrs Shaefer yawned loudly and stood up. She said, 'I've heard all this before,' and left the room. After a moment the others followed, leaving Rose alone at the table with Jesse. He asked, 'Are you sure you want to hear this?'

She said, 'Only if you don't mind telling me. I don't want to be a burden.'

'It's an important piece of history,' he said, 'a piece that will determine our future. People need to be aware of consequences.'

He was very sure of himself; she watched his hand reaching back to finger his ponytail.

'He returned to Memphis on April fourth, a Thursday, and checked into the Lorraine Hotel. He'd been criticised for staying only in the best hotels, so he chose one less likely to cause offence. He was in his room, 306, most of the day, talking about his beliefs. I guess he knew what was going to happen.'

'Gosh,' breathed Rose.

'He said he had conquered the fear of death, and that though he would like to live a long life . . . longevity had its grace . . . he wasn't concerned about that now, he just wanted to do God's will. God had allowed him to go up the mountain and he'd looked over and seen the promised land.'

Rose kept silent. He sounded very religious.

'Round about six o'clock he stepped out onto the balcony. Someone pointed out a man in the crowd below who was going to play the organ in the church he was due to speak in that night. King said, "Oh yeah, he's my man. Tell him to play 'Precious Lord', and to play it real pretty."'

Rose stared at him and didn't see him. Dr Wheeler had taken his place, was watching her.

She was eleven years old, crouched down beside the ditch, examining a spent bullet she'd found in the mud. She knew who he was, though he was so ancient he was all but invisible. He lived in the house with a turret beyond the railway crossing. His wife wore a daft panama hat and rode a bicycle; whenever she went to the chip shop in Brows Lane she hooked

31

a basket onto the handlebars, so as not to be seen taking her supper home in a newspaper. He said, 'If you hold an object that close to your eyes, you shut out the rest of the world.' She said, 'Yes, thank you,' because that's how you replied to the elderly.

'King was leaning out over the rail of the balcony. As he straightened up the shot was fired.'

He spoke to her again, a year later, in winter. He wore a duffle coat and a grey trilby hat. She had a stick and was trying to impale a dead frog clamped in the iced-over rain pools below the pine woods.

'He slumped down, sprawled against the rail,' said Shaefer.

'What are you doing?' he asked. 'Stabbing frogs,' she said. 'They're not frogs,' he corrected. 'They're Natterjack toads.'

Harold came into the room. 'I'm nearly through,' Shaefer assured him. 'Everything OK out there?'

'Dandy,' Harold said. 'Bud's going on about the time we went to camp and Mason Junior took a shot at that bear. He left out the part when he screamed and jumped into the river.'

Shaefer sniggered. Harold pocketed a pill bottle beside the salt cellar and went out again. He didn't look at Rose.

'He had a fountain pen in his top pocket,' said Shaefer. He pointed at the cup beside the stuffed owl. 'When he fell, it flipped out and rolled into a corner.'

The following month she saw him again, though no words passed between them. On impulse, she turned left after the railway crossing and followed the cinder path that led to the coal trucks beside the powerhouse. It was not somewhere she often went. For a while she clambered in and out of the trucks and threw pieces of coal into the tunnel. Then she found an old hammer in the sand and a wooden ammunition box with a splintered lid. She pretended she was in Occupied France, on the run from the Germans and in contact with the Resistance. 'Tommy Handley . . . Tommy Handley,' she tapped out, 'Can I do you now, sir?' It was a secret code and meant she needed a signal to detonate her bombs. Now it began to rain, first merely a sprinkle, then a downpour. As she was about to run for the tunnel, she tapped, 'I am alone . . . wait . . . wait . . . danger . . . I am not alone.'

Shaefer said, 'He was kind of frozen, except for the blood gushing from a massive tear in his neck.'

Afterwards, she stood so long in the open and got so wet that she felt God was cleansing her. The thump of her heart mimicked the forlorn boom of the buoy tossing on the horizon of the glistening sea. When she hurled the hammer from her, it swooped into the sandhills like a bird of prey. She entered the tunnel and began to wobble on tiptoe along the metal rail, and stopped; a figure stood dark against the exit. Then it turned, and for a moment a face was illuminated in apricot light and she recognised Dr Wheeler. Then he was gone.

Shaefer said, 'We knew he'd had it.'

She was a yard away from emerging onto the shore when her foot touched an obstruction piled against the rail. Peering closer, she saw it was Billy Rotten, the recluse who lived in a driftwood shack in the pine woods. Black slime slithered from his ear. He looked at her, eyes fearful, and raised a hand to touch her mouth. Then his body sagged. She tasted moisture on her lips and licked away blood. She said, 'I'm sorry, Mr Billy,' and scurried on.

'One could tell by his eyes . . .' Shaefer said.

Because of the First World War, Mr Billy wasn't himself and it wasn't wise to go too near. He suffered from shell shock, an affliction brought on by lumps of earth from the trenches blowing into his brain. In time, so Mother had told her, this had developed into Perversion, a mystery disease which impelled him to get hold of children and stick something inside them which could cause an explosion.

'. . . they were wide open, but they weren't seeing anything.'

She ran out of the tunnel and didn't look back. Now the sea was swallowing the blood-red sun and the world was darkening. In the dying light the marram grasses flickered in silver strips across the shifting dunes. Above the black hulk of the powerhouse appeared the twinkle of a first star. There was no sign of Dr Wheeler.

'It was a white man who killed him,' said Shaefer.

She never told anybody she'd seen Dr Wheeler that night, not even when the vicar called round to see Mother about the Amateur Dramatics supper night and she'd asked him if the butcher boy was right when he held that Billy Rotten had been the victim of a bayonet stabbing. The vicar said he was not right at all, that he'd been informed by George Rimmer, the coalman, that Mr Rotten had died from being battered on his head. They'd found a hammer in the sand. Once started, the vicar grew lachrymose; eyes shiny with moisture, he discussed conscience and how whoever was responsible for such a misdemeanour would never find peace, either in this world or the next.

'It wasn't a killing based on hatred,' said Shaefer, 'simply an attempt to draw attention to the problems of our time.'

'Of course,' said Rose.

Shaefer blew his nose before helping her upright. It's only people who are comfortably off, Rose thought, who can afford to be upset about coloured people. She could smell flowers as he propelled her into the room with the settees. Beyond the glass doors a crimson sunset leaked across the sky. Bud or Bob was parading the floor, shoulders hunched, arm extended. 'Bang, bang,' he shouted, voice raised above the hooting turmoil in the street below.

Rose, fighting sleep, found herself slumped beside the woman in the Bermuda shorts; she asked her why Harold took pills.

'His stomach,' said Thora. 'He suffers from gas.' She put an arm round Rose and shook her. Leaning closer she whispered, 'I guess it was a blow . . . not finding Fred.'

'Fred,' echoed Rose.

'Wheeler,' Thora said. Even though the day was fading her plump knees reflected light.

'You knew him?' cried Rose.

'Sssh,' hissed Thora. She straightened up and smiled vacuously at Harold who had turned to look at them.

It was Jesse Shaefer who suggested that Rose should stay the night. He reckoned Harold wouldn't care to leave the camper unattended in the underground garage, not if there was stuff on the roof, but there was no need for Rose to lose out on a proper bed. His wife agreed. Harold just nodded.

At some point of darkness candles were lit, sending shadows fleeing across the ceiling. Harold began a story about a man who was responsible for someone's death, even though his finger hadn't been on the trigger. Rose couldn't see his whole face, only his lips spitting words above the fuzz of his beard.

'Mrs Stanford,' she interrupted, 'was very discreet. She never mentioned her dead husband.'

Mrs Shaefer escorted her to a room with a poster on the wall depicting a boy with very little hair playing baseball.

'I'm not myself,' Rose confided. 'It's being away from home. And Harold's not easy. I'm not even sure he likes me.'

'You'll feel differently in the morning,' George said. 'Sleep solves most things.'

'He's very bossy,' Rose insisted. 'Very sure of himself.'

'Strange you should think that,' said George, pushing her on to the bed. 'A man more unsure of himself would be hard to find.'

'I can't undress,' Rose protested, tugging off her shoes and scrabbling under the sheets. 'I'm shy with strangers. We never undressed at home.'

'No problem,' said Mrs Shaefer.

'That lady in the short trousers,' Rose murmured, grazing sleep, 'she said she knew Dr Wheeler.'

'We all did,' responded Mrs Shaefer, heaving the counterpane into place as though it were a shroud.

*   *   *

Harold woke early and took one of his tablets to be on the safe side. His belly pains had miraculously disappeared when he'd met Dollie, and returned once she'd left. His mother, a strong woman, hadn't believed in stomach disorders. Such malfunctions, she reasoned, originated in the brains of those unwilling to face reality; her first husband had developed colitis after the crash of 1929.

He checked that the tarpaulin hadn't been tampered with. As a precaution he dug out the cardboard box and, removing it from its pillowcase, thrust it under the driving seat. His hand touched paper; it was the news cutting previously pinned to the back of his bedroom door in Baltimore. Stuffing it into his pocket he went upstairs to the apartment. Rose was still asleep.

Jesse cooked him breakfast. Both he and George voiced concern at what he intended to do. They said it was a pity the confrontation couldn't take place in Washington, where the two of them might be of help. Three heads were better than one. After all, nearly five years had passed, and it hadn't all been Wheeler's fault. There were wrongs on both sides.

'You could at least stay a couple of nights more,' said George. 'It's my birthday on Thursday.'

'She's forty-six again,' said Jesse.

'I have to see him,' Harold protested. 'There's things I have to say.'

It wasn't the truth. There were no words left and even if he could find them they would stick in his throat. Before meeting Dollie he'd been a reasonable sort of man, to the point of dullness. He had no illusions in that regard. As a boy he'd been described as reserved, which was a kinder way of putting it. Dollie's involvement with him had astonished everybody, himself most of all. They had tried to warn him. Bud had taken him aside that time in the men's room of Monticello's restaurant and asked him, tactfully enough, if he knew what he

37

was getting into. He'd shouted he didn't care and Bud had cautioned that passion was a two-edged sword. It could pierce the mind as well as the heart.

Jesse, planting a plate of fried eggs on the table, said it was odd that Wheeler hadn't written the girl a proper letter, merely supplied an address. It was as though he was playing a game.

'When did he ever do anything else?' remarked George.

Neither of them could fathom Wheeler's friendship with Rose. She was far from his usual type of female. George thought she was verging on the simple.

'The British have a different approach to things,' defended Jesse. 'I come across it all the time. I guess it has to do with a culture founded on isolation . . . the isolation of an island people.'

'She told me,' George said, 'that her father had ruined her life and that her mother had died from injections usually given to horses.'

Jesse argued it was the gin. And Rose was very young, hardly more than a child.

George said, 'Her father knew Wheeler and called him a crook. Apparently they lived in the same street. They almost came to fisticuffs once, something to do with a seat on a train. She came out with this cockamamie story in the middle of a discussion with Bob about Johnson ordering more troops to Vietnam.'

'She's older than you think,' said Harold. 'She's nearly thirty.'

He discussed the route to Wanakena. It was his intention to make for Jersey City and then follow the line of the Hudson River through Poughkeepsie, Rhinebeck, Ravena; at Corinth he'd stop off to see Chip Webster. Jesse expressed surprise that he was still in touch with Webster. He hadn't realised they were that friendly.

'We're not,' Harold said.

George thought it a pity he was going to bypass New York. Think of the girl coming all this way and then to miss out on Ellis Island. The British were suckers for the past.

Harold said, 'I doubt Rose has ever heard of Ellis Island. The only past that interests her is her own.'

When Rose joined them, he was taken aback by her appearance. Though her clothes were even more creased, her face had altered. It wasn't that she had become pretty, just that he hadn't noticed until now the arch of dark eyebrows beneath her fluff of pale hair.

She said, addressing George, 'I want to apologise for the way I behaved last night. I was out of order.'

George waved a dismissive hand. 'Not as wayward as Bud,' she said. 'He threw up in the elevator.'

'I had a strange dream,' said Rose, 'about Dr Wheeler. He was walking through a cemetery, writing down names.'

There was no response. Jesse fiddled with the coffee percolator. Harold stared down at the road map; he was remembering a morning in high summer, birdsong in the trees, the flicker of insects above a lake glossy under sunlight. 'I do love you,' she'd protested and, sick with fear, he'd told her that love was not the problem. Love dropped out of the sky, unsought, unearned. He had loved his mother. It was liking somebody that was difficult.

George asked, 'Does Wheeler know you're

travelling with Harold?'

'Not really,' said Rose. 'I did write to tell him I'd met a nice American, but I didn't give a name because Harold never mentioned he knew him, not until much later. And by the time he did, Dr Wheeler had left Chicago. I don't think he could have got my next letter.'

'It's an interesting fact,' George said, 'that if you want to know your real opinion of anyone you should notice the impression made by their handwriting on the envelope.'

'Time's getting on,' Harold interrupted, folding his map.

George asked Rose what she wanted for breakfast. She said, 'Nothing, thank you, not after last night's huge meal.' Jesse handed her an apple, large and red, which she bit into boisterously.

During the goodbyes, Rose kissed George Shaefer's cheek. Lifting the hem of her apron, George dabbed it away. Jesse, walking his guests to the elevator, urged Harold to keep in touch. 'Phone any time,' he insisted, embracing him. Harold hugged him back, which surprised them both. 'There, there,' Jesse muttered, patting his shoulder.

Approaching the camper, Rose hurled her half-eaten apple across the garage floor. Its bounce echoed from the concrete walls. Harold clenched his fists but said nothing. He had a picture in his head of abandoning her at midnight on some deserted highway; increasing speed, he'd watch her image dwindle in a mirror bright with moonshine.

Before leaving Washington he drove along Wisconsin Avenue where, years before, he had shared a two-roomed apartment with Chip Webster. The house looked much the same, save

40

that the branches of the once newly planted maple tree now swayed above its roof. He told Rose he had lived on the ground floor, and she asked if he had been happy there. 'Happy?' he repeated, as though it was a word in a foreign tongue. Then she explained that she had thrown the apple away as she wasn't used to fruit, on account of rationing in her childhood. He was taken aback; it amounted to an apology.

CHAPTER FOUR

They travelled along what Harold referred to as an interstate highway. Rose, aware that her apple throwing had annoyed him, told him how much she'd liked the Shaefers. She thought it would please him if she praised his friends. 'It was nice,' she enthused, 'the way they didn't flare up when drink was spilled or ash got flicked onto the carpet.'

'Don't kid yourself,' Harold retorted. 'Disorder brings Jesse out in a rash. The poor guy probably spent half the night tidying up the mess.'

Then he told her, politely enough, to keep quiet, that he needed to concentrate. She said she quite understood, the traffic being so dense, and he said it wasn't the cars, more that he had a lot on his mind.

She didn't mind not talking; it wasn't as if he understood what she was on about. She filled her mind with images of Dr Wheeler, hand beginning to rise, the day they had said goodbye at Charing Cross train station.

After a while, two hours perhaps, the cars

41

thinned out and they drove through countryside, the fields stretching to the horizon and a tractor, bulky yellow, going up and over a brown hill. They sped past houses with verandas with chairs set out, washing stiff on a rope between trees, sun reflecting silver bright off the tin roof of an outhouse, and a dream sequence flash of a family leaning on wooden railings, Ma, Pa and idiot daughter, head as big as a pumpkin. Next came a sign indicating the New Jersey Turnpike and later a bridge. Now Harold slowed down. It was very hot; when he shook his head sweat sprayed the window glass. Then he brought the van to a halt. Looking up she saw a landscape of blackened warehouses, set amidst rubble speared with electric pylons, cables sagging below the sky. There were cranes and bulldozers without any workers. Beyond the bonnet of the van a rusted army truck lay on its side, jolted seats splaying prehistoric wings.

'It's like the docks at Liverpool,' she said, 'when the war was over.'

'It's in the process of regeneration,' he said, and urged her out. He said they were in Caven Point Road and he needed to show her something of importance. She had to do what he wanted because without him she wouldn't find Dr Wheeler.

There was a breeze coming from somewhere ahead, which must have made him feel good because he linked arms with her as though they were pals. She felt a bit awkward trying to keep in step, but was relieved things were getting better between them.

Stealing a sideways glance at the shine of his balding head, his boy's face with its inappropriate beard, it struck her that he was in disguise. All his

42

fussing over baths and toothbrushes was a front to hide the real Harold, the one she hadn't yet discovered. It was his much-married mother, she reckoned, who was the cause of the problem.

Often, when she had whinged about Father, Dr Wheeler had quoted lines written by a man called Pound, something to do with a family unable to have order if the father had not order within him. It was supposed to be a poem, but it didn't rhyme.

All children were the product of domination by their parents, girls as well as boys, although she herself was an exception. She never had been, not even when threatened. Once, when Father had sworn at her, she'd waited until he retreated into the scullery, then leapt on his back, arm about his throat, and wrestled him to the ground. She'd known how to do it from seeing commandos in action in war films.

They walked up a slope of ground to where, so Harold informed her, the Upper Bay met the Hudson River. Across the swollen water reared a shimmering giant, one arm scraping the heavens. Harold said it was the Statue of Liberty and that the blurred outline behind was Manhattan Island.

That night, they stayed in a camping area near a lake. According to Harold the site wasn't typical of its kind, having degenerated into a permanent home for migrant workers laid off years before over some dispute to do with steel production. There were places like this all over America, he said, mainly to do with the decline in farming and a subsequent mass exodus to the cities. Trailers propped on bricks and patrolled by skinny dogs occupied most of the spaces. Alongside a lean-to shack selling strong drink, firelighters and logs, there was a hut with toilet facilities.

Harold ordered her into the encircling trees to gather twigs; he didn't approve of firelighters, not when he was rubbing shoulders with nature. She hadn't minded; woods were a habitat she felt comfortable in. From the lake beyond came the squawking of wild geese.

Earlier that day he had bought slices of steak from a shop called the Darling Boy Diner. When the fire had caught, he impaled the meat on a spit and instructed her to keep turning it while he went off to the washroom. He came back in striped pyjamas, under a dressing gown with his initials embroidered on the breast pocket.

When she'd eaten, Rose followed his example. The bulb in the washroom ceiling was faulty and there were dead insects splattered across the concrete walls. Washed all over, she scurried back in her nightgown and raincoat to find an agitated man talking to Harold. Their conversation was difficult to follow because the man kept coughing and hawking up sputum. Harold nodded a lot and said little beyond interjecting that time had a way of slotting things into perspective. Rose thought he was talking rubbish. The man had no teeth and a glob of congealed blood on his temple. Before staggering off he tried to kiss Harold's hand. Harold backed away, as if in touch with leprosy.

'You were nasty,' Rose protested. 'Couldn't you see he was in pain?'

'Who isn't?' he snapped.

Interrogated, he said the poor man was depressed, short of money. He hadn't given him any, it would have only gone on drink. Rose thought this was stingy, him being so rich he didn't

44

even have to work. She knew that from George Shaefer who, when prodded, had told her she was mistaken in thinking Harold was a psychologist. He was interested in that sort of thing, she'd said, for obvious reasons, but his money came from investments.

They remained beside the fire until midnight, facing each other through the cascade of sparks spat from the burning wood, listening to the sudden furious barking of dogs and the intermittent drumming of cicadas.

She needn't have worried about lying down next to him in the darkness of the van. He'd slept with his back to her, and once, when she'd turned over and her body brushed against his, he'd immediately twisted away.

*　　　*　　　*

The following morning Harold went for a swim in the nearby lake. He wanted her to join him, but she told him she couldn't swim. She could tell from his expression that he didn't believe her. She started to tell him about the time she'd been shoved into the pond in the school playground, but he walked off in the middle. When he was out of sight, she climbed into the van and ferreted inside the cardboard box under the driver's seat. She didn't touch the gun, just looked at it.

When Harold returned he changed into shorts. They were quite long and baggy but when he sat down at the wheel she saw the freckles on his knees.

After two hours they drove into a rural landscape with mountains, damson coloured, rolling against the sky. Sometimes the road was cut out of rock splashing metallic blue in the sunlight. At a turning near a house without a roof they almost ran over a large hen which Harold identified as a wild turkey. It wasn't scared, just stood there gobbling outrage.

That evening they struck camp on the outskirts of an oak wood. This time there was a proper café and Harold, confessing he was too tired and dehydrated to mess about with fires, insisted they should eat there. Rose made excuses, protesting she wasn't hungry, but he took no notice. Gripping her elbow he marched her through the doors. Earlier that day he'd asked if she wanted to buy anything and she'd said she needed stamps for the postcards she'd bought in London. When she handed him some money he wouldn't take it. She felt bad; she didn't like sponging off him, not when she wasn't going to give him anything in return.

While waiting for the meal to be served she took one of the postcards out of her handbag, a portrait of Queen Elizabeth and her sister Margaret taken when they were children. Both of them had hair screwed up into curls. She'd chosen it because it had reminded her of the day she'd defied Mother and refused point blank to go to Mrs Formby's shop in the village to undergo a permanent wave. From the age of five Mother had been trying to make her look like Shirley Temple. Never again, she'd shouted, would she submit to those heated canisters that belched smoke and singed her hair into sausage shapes. When it rained she knew she smelt funny. The girls at school said she ponged like someone dragged from a bonfire.

Harold asked if she had something to write with. She said, 'Yes, thank you,' and took a long time over Polly and Bernard's address. Then she scribbled, *Lovely weather . . . America is amazing.* She couldn't write down her real thoughts, not when Harold might want to read them. As the waitress delivered the food to the table, he said, 'That pen . . . where did you get it?'

She replied, quickly enough, 'It was my father's. It was presented to him when he retired from the Corn Exchange, in recognition of his allegiance to commerce.'

She ate looking out of the window because Harold was a messy eater. He munched even his potatoes to a pulp, as though in danger of choking. And he flicked his tongue in and out of his teeth.

Later, he busied himself fitting up a mosquito net so that they could sleep with the doors open. It was still very close and Rose could feel her hair sticking to her scalp. She climbed into the front seat to fetch her towel and bottle of shampoo. Harold's jacket was draped over the steering wheel, a fold of paper sticking up from the pocket. Telling him she wouldn't be long, she went to the shower room attached to the café. Hair washed, she walked into the shade of the oak trees and crouched there, head between her knees, towelling it dry.

It was very still in the wood; sometimes a dagger of sunlight pierced the leaves, spattering the brown earth with silver. When she'd brushed her hair straight, she examined the newspaper cutting removed from Harold's jacket. The sentence *Prominent lawyer commits suicide* was printed beneath the blurred photograph of a woman's face. There was no name, no further information. Rummaging in her bag for the fountain pen she'd used earlier, she wrapped it in the piece of paper and hurled it into the undergrowth. Then she

47

walked back to the van.

Harold had brought out two canvas stools for them to perch on. He'd opened a bottle of wine; it was already half empty. She didn't blame him. It couldn't be easy spending time with someone who, in spite of a shared language, amounted to a foreigner—and a smoker into the bargain. He handed her a glass but she shook her head. She wasn't into wine; in her opinion it took far too long to make one feel cheerful.

Harold had been reading a book, yet for once he seemed anxious to talk. He even paid her a sort of compliment, to do with her hair looking shiny; he said it rippled like a flag in the wind. She blushed in spite of herself. Then he told her that in the morning, at a place called Corinth, he intended to call on a man he had once shared an apartment with when young.

'A friend?' she asked, though she knew; she remembered the house pointed at when leaving Washington.

He said, 'Once . . . not any more. Something interfered. He let me down.'

She said, 'We always think that, don't we, when things don't go the way we want? He was probably only doing what he felt he needed to do.'

She was thinking of Dr Wheeler's explanation of why people behaved badly. Little men, he'd told her, who gained advantages by performing devious acts were no different from the mighty wrongdoers. Napoleon had been no more culpable than those who possessed the same wish to harm, except that he'd had the power. It had to do with the need to be in control, plus a steady heartbeat which fuelled the will to live; she hadn't altogether understood

48

that last bit.

'Someone died,' Harold said. He was looking at her properly now, the way people did when pain needed to be shared. Suddenly he raised his hand and slapped his cheek so violently that he sagged sideways on his stool. 'Jesus,' he cried.

'I'm worried,' she blurted out, 'as to the passage of time. I'm due back at work in three weeks. How many days will it take us to get to that Wanathingee place?'

'Twenty-four hours,' he muttered, scratching his bitten face.

She was astonished. It seemed to her that her old life, the one in London, had been lived so long ago that time had bounced out of control, like a stone ricocheting down a hill.

Harold clambered into the van and returned with a bottle of insect repellent and two photographs, one of a man with a head of black hair digging a hole in a garden, and another of the same man arm in arm with a woman with a big bosom. 'Of course,' he said, punching a cloud of spray into the air, 'his face would have been ageing when you knew him.' Then he rambled on about his first impressions of Wheeler: his smile edged with sarcasm, the way he had of clearing his throat, the stories he'd told about his childhood in Oregon. Had he told her his father had been a member of the Senate, and before that a drinking companion of Ezra Pound, a poet who went mad? Pound had given him a watch with a strap made out of crocodile skin.

'I've never heard of Mr Pound,' she said, handing back the photographs. 'And I never saw Dr Wheeler's hair . . . he always wore a trilby.'

'Didn't you think him somewhat secretive, not

49

the easiest of men to get to know?'

'No,' she said. 'He was more easy than anyone I've ever met.'

Still, he wouldn't give up. 'Did you think of him as a substitute father?' he demanded.

'Never,' she shouted.

Behind Washington Harold's head the sun was sinking, smudging the horizon with pink. From somewhere beyond the trees came the melancholy strumming of a guitar. Rose, eyes pricking tears, saw Father's face, the yellowing cheekbones, the colourless lips, the open wound on his temple never healed from bashing against the iron mantelpiece when stooping to poke the fire.

That night she'd come back from the shore, he'd been sitting in the dark listening to the Saturday night play. He'd wedged the blue satin cushion on the floor beneath the window, in case of sabotage to the wireless balanced on the narrow shelf above. There was an aerial strung between the house wall and next door's fence, and often Mother forgot what the wire was for and slung the string mat over it before washing out the scullery. Then the wireless would leap off the ledge and Father, ranting and raving, would get out the sticky tape. She was pushing past his chair to go into the hall when he said, aping surprise, Good heavens! If it isn't the Constant Nymph. She replied, coldly enough, Could be . . . you never know who'll pop in, and was turning the handle of the door when he sat upright and said, Wait on, I want a word. She slouched against the door and avoided looking at him; he was wearing his Home Guard beret. I've been thinking, Rose, he said, what to get you for your birthday. Is there anything you really want? She said, Not really, which was a lie. She would have liked a

50

watch with a strap made of crocodile skin.

Harold said, 'Wheeler was very keen on Paris. He even talked of us both going there some day. He'd once lived for a year in a room in the rue Jacob. Did he ever talk of Paris to you?'

Your mother, Father said, and cleared his throat as though the word had caused an irritation, mentioned a charm bracelet. That was last year, she told him. I'm off charm bracelets now. Well, give it a thought, he said. Humiliated, he leaned forward and kicked the coals into flame.

'He was a great man for firing the imagination,' said Harold. 'Not good, however, at following things through. All sound and no impact.'

The blast of a gunshot followed her down the hall, then a thin scream. Someone always died in the Saturday play, and never from natural causes. She hadn't bothered going into Mother's room to say goodnight. She wouldn't be back yet. She was down at the railway station reading her library book by the fire in the waiting room; it was where she went every night until Father returned to normal.

Rose went to bed before Washington Harold. From the trees beyond came the sound of barking. Bernard and Polly had a boxer dog, and as she sank into sleep it leapt up to lick her hand.

At some hour in the darkness she was conscious of Harold patting her back; deep down she knew that he wasn't trying to wake her, simply imitating her heartbeat to be of comfort.

51

CHAPTER FIVE

They were driving along a deserted highway some miles beyond Poughkeepsie when Harold became aware of a rattling sound. It wasn't thunderous, more like dice being shaken. He couldn't locate where it came from and prodded Rose to find out if she too could hear it. As usual she was slumped in her seat, eyes hidden behind her sunglasses.

'Hear what?' she asked.

'Something rattling . . . or shaking.'

'I wasn't listening . . . I've been trying to remember a poem.'

He applied the brakes and climbed out to look under the hood. He could see nothing wrong save for a weak spiral of steam, but then he knew little about engines.

As soon as he drove on the rattling began again. 'Can't you hear it now?' he demanded.

'No,' Rose said. 'It's possibly an interior disorder . . . in you, I mean. Or maybe a fly has flown into your ear. It happened to me once, but it was a wasp.'

He told himself that if he wanted to avoid slapping her he must bear in mind that he was dealing with a retard. The sun was now at its height and there was no breeze to cool his face. Sweat ran down his forehead. Seeing a blur of trees on the horizon he increased his speed; the rattling increased in volume. Half an hour later he drew into the shadows of a wood.

'Before him like a blood-red flag, the bright flamingoes flew,' Rose intoned as she stepped out after him.

He unlocked the back of the camper and climbed inside to examine its contents. Everything appeared secure. Out of breath, he lay on his stomach, chin resting on his folded arms, watching Rose as she lolled against a pine tree, a cigarette between her fingers, hair clinging damply to her neck. At last he said, 'You must have heard something? You did, didn't you?' As always when he wished to assert himself, his tone of voice was plaintive.

'Yes,' she replied, 'I did. But vans always rattle. Besides, I knew you were getting upset.'

Any day now, he thought, he'd show her what upset really meant. Soon after, the heat must have put him to sleep. When he woke it was almost dark, but that was because the mosquito net had been lowered to protect him from the sun. It was considerate of Rose to have done that.

They were passing through the village of Rhinebeck when she shouted for him to stop. Harold thought she'd noticed the Victorian-style houses, but she said she'd spotted a church and that she felt like praying. Bemused, he watched her running back down the sidewalk.

The night before, he'd commented on the way she drummed her fingers on her knees when listening to the radio and she'd said she'd been good at playing the piano, until her mother had battered her knuckles with a spoon whenever she struck a wrong note. That, he'd said, sure was a dumb way to encourage a love of music, and she'd retorted that piano lessons cost a lot of money, and anyway she preferred the ukulele. He couldn't make out her attitude to her mother, or to anyone else for that matter. Later, she came out with a

53

confusing story about being off school for a week and how, by way of excuse, she'd told Miss Albright, her teacher, that there'd been a tragedy in the family, that her mother had committed suicide. 'Oh God,' he'd cried, the insect bite on his cheek flaring up and his heart missing a beat. And then, seeing the expression on his face, she'd said that her mother hadn't done any such thing and that she'd fibbed on account of Miss Albright having just lost her sweetheart in the Battle of Britain. 'Something,' she said, 'was needed to take her mind off things.'

He wanted to tell Rose she needed a psychiatrist, but the wine had addled him. When he got into bed he'd tried to wake her by tapping her back. He would have climbed on top of her, more out of spite than desire, but the crackle of burning wood distracted him. It wasn't wise to leave the fire unattended.

When Rose returned from the church, he foolishly asked if she was religious and she snapped that she could be if the place was right. He didn't understand what she meant until she moaned about the absence of candles and proper statues. He was about to remind her that such fripperies had nothing to do with belief, but thought better of it.

Stopping the camper on the outskirts of Corinth he sat in silence, tapping the steering wheel with his fist. He'd visited the town once before, as a child. He had no pictorial memories of the place, merely sounds, that of raised voices accompanying an abrupt departure from a house as the sun was climbing to destroy the darkness.

Presently Rose nudged his arm. She asked if he'd lost his way. He told her that his stepfather's sister had once lived nearby. 'There was an argument,' he said. 'I was asleep. Back then, I didn't understand what it was about.'

Rose asked if he'd been frightened, shaken from his bed without explanation. She herself, she said, had spent most of her childhood crouched on the stairs listening to her parents calling each other names. 'It was scary,' she said, 'but it made me strong.'

He couldn't agree with her. 'This aunt was six foot,' he confided, 'with eyes the colour of steel.'

'So what?' she replied.

'It shattered me,' he blurted, and instantly regretted his choice of words. He didn't want her to think of him as a man in pieces.

Chip Webster's house was on a tree-lined street with white flowers wilting on the porch. Next door, a woman with red hair stood on tiptoe pruning a rose bush. Harold sat for a long time, staring at a dog sniffing at a newspaper on the sloping lawn. For once, Rose kept her mouth shut. Minutes passed, and then the door opened and a man sprinted down the steps and approached the mailbox. He was barefooted and wearing nothing but a bathrobe. His neighbour nodded at him and he shouted something, at which she clicked her fingers to entice the dog back into her house. It took no notice.

'That's him,' Harold said, and stayed put.

'It would be best,' said Rose, 'if you stopped thinking of how it used to be and just concentrated on the now.'

She was right, of course, but then she didn't know about his particular past. 'Stay here,' he said, and climbed out.

Chip Webster was about to slam the door behind

him when Harold mounted the steps. Chip said, 'Long time no see,' and added, looking at the camper, 'bring her in.' It was obvious Jesse Shaefer had telephoned ahead.

Reluctantly, he beckoned for Rose to follow. She bounded onto the sidewalk, flinging her raincoat behind her, breasts jiggling.

The front room needed a coat of paint. Damp mutilated the left-hand wall. Above the mantel of the open door, leading onto a back porch, hung an enlarged photograph, its frame garlanded with long-dead flowers. There were two plates on the table, one messy with the remains of a meal, and a torn loaf next to a joint of meat perilously close to a ginger cat slurping liquid from a soup bowl. A woman sat on the stairs, rocking backwards and forwards; she was either humming or sobbing and wore men's pyjamas. The big toes of her bare feet were painted scarlet. Harold made a move towards her, from politeness, but her eyes, outlined in smeared mascara, were full of hostility.

Webster didn't bother to introduce her, just came out with the usual remarks: pleasant journey, changeable weather, how they were all getting older. Looking at him, Harold could see little truth in that last observation. Webster's hair was as dark as it had always been, his gaze as penetrating. He showed no signs of unease at this sudden, if forewarned, visitation. When he sat down, his bathrobe didn't quite cover the bulge of his testicles. A man so sure of himself, reasoned Harold, was incapable of feeling exposed.

From day one, Webster had known what Wheeler was up to, had lied on his behalf. Once, coming out of a bar in downtown Washington the

56

worse for drink, he'd gone halfway to spelling out what was happening. But then, despite prodding, he'd clammed up. Later, it became obvious that he'd been a willing go-between, had even allowed his address to be used for letters. Worse, when that final act of abandonment was attempted, it was Webster who was informed of its awful conclusion.

Webster and Rose hit it off immediately. He told her to help herself to food; twice, stepping over the humming woman, he went upstairs, first to fetch a bottle of wine, then a bottle-opener. He mustn't have been concentrating because there was a corkscrew next to the bread.

Rose hacked at the meat and tugged clumps from the loaf as though she was starving. They had stopped an hour before in order to eat, but she'd insisted the piece of fried bread she'd consumed earlier was quite sufficient. When she'd gobbled herself to a halt she took one of Webster's cigarettes and they both sat there, blowing smoke at the stained ceiling. The cat had taken a fancy to her; it curled round her shoulder, one paw against her throat. Once again, as in days gone by, Harold felt he was invisible.

Webster asked Rose if she'd found the journey across the state exciting, stimulating. She didn't lie. She said she wasn't interested in landscapes or towns, that she hadn't noticed where she was, only paid attention to what was going on in her head. She'd been trying to recall a piece of poetry she'd once learned, about a coloured man who was having a dream of the life he'd led before becoming a slave; Webster grimaced, but she didn't notice. She did remember passing through a place with houses outlined in fairy lights, like it was Christmas,

57

and hadn't seen the point of that, seeing it was summer. Webster thumped the table with his fist and shouted she was right . . . she was right. He struck so violently that the cat leapt off Rose and fled in terror. Suddenly the woman on the stairs laughed, shrill as glass breaking.

For a moment no one spoke, then Webster got up from the table and hauling the woman to her feet propelled her up the stairs.

'Trouble at mill,' whispered Rose obtusely.

Harold studied the photograph within the faded flowers. It portrayed Bud Holland, Webster, Bob Maitland and Jesse Shaefer kneeling, youthfully grinning, on a baseball pitch. He himself, as always, stood in the background, face bereft of expression.

'Are you in that?' Rose asked.

'Not that you'd notice,' he said, and walked out onto the porch. Ahead of him, across a wooden fence, a small boy encased in diamond sunlight knelt beside a toy truck. A little girl skipped towards him carrying a bucket and, tripping, sloshed water over the boy's knees. He jumped up and shoved her to the ground; face crumpled, she let out a wail of despair.

Hearing voices behind him Harold went indoors. Suddenly he knew it wouldn't do any good to stir up the past, certainly not in front of Rose. Nothing would bring Dollie back.

Rose was sitting at the table, gazing up at Webster, mouth open. He was squeezing her shoulder and looking serious. Harold said, 'Everything all right?'

'Nothing I can't handle,' said Webster.

Small talk followed, mostly about the route they should take towards Saratoga Springs, and then

58

Rose mentioned that the van was making a funny noise. Webster offered to take a look at the engine. Harold protested that it wasn't necessary, that he'd find a gas station, but already Webster was opening the door.

The dog was still on the lawn, scrabbling at the grass with its paws. Head under the hood of the camper, Webster said, 'Shaefer's worried about you, you know.'

'He's a good friend,' Harold replied.

'We both think you're a fool to go to Wanakena. It won't solve anything.'

'So what?' he said, kicking the gravel and wishing it was Webster.

'Have you forgotten what happened when Bud took on his Pa?'

Harold did remember. Bud had been left a large sum of money by his mother. His father had contested the will on the grounds that his son was too young for such wealth and would probably drink himself into the grave. Bud won. His father, hopelessly in debt, threw himself from the twenty-ninth floor of the SunLife Insurance building. After that Bud drank like a fish.

Harold said, 'I have to see Wheeler.'

'It won't do no good.'

'Lots of things don't do no good,' he retorted. 'Including the part you played.'

Webster shot up and slammed the hood down. 'Anyone else,' he shouted, 'unless fucking blind and deaf would have known what was going on.'

'You were my friend too,' Harold said, and heard the whine in his voice. The dog bounded towards them, barking.

'Fuck off,' bawled Webster; he wasn't talking to

the dog. Seizing Harold by the shoulders he sent him sprawling. A bunch of keys jerked onto the grass.

What happened next was embarrassing. Rose ran down the steps and, enfolding him in her arms, shouted at Webster to go away. Her lips were on his cheek, breath musky with tobacco smoke. She wriggled two fingers behind his ear, scrabbling at his skin as though it was the cat she held. Cradled there, Harold reminded himself that women were programmed to show sympathy, not rationally, merely from need.

After a conciliatory handshake with Webster, he strode towards the camper, followed almost immediately by a hasty return and an undignified crawl on all fours in search of the spilled keys.

CHAPTER SIX

The journey continued down shimmering roads bordered by curly trees. Miraculously, or because of Webster, the thumping of the engine had gone away.

Rose felt considerably more at ease now that she'd actually touched Harold. He didn't show it, but she sensed the animosity between them had shrunk. It was a bit like the shyness one felt before having sex and the familiarity let loose once it had happened. She'd always been uncomfortable during preliminaries, hadn't known how to behave, swum free when penetration happened, experienced a tearful relief when love evaporated like steam puffing from a kettle.

60

For all their new understanding, she still thought Harold a funny man. For some time he parroted on about how badly Webster had behaved to the woman on the stairs with the painted toenails. He'd obviously let his lover down, he said, treated her with a lack of respect. Rose felt obliged to point out that only women had lovers, not men; Dr Wheeler, being an educated man, had corrected her on that score after she'd mentioned her involvement with a bulky professor of physics. Besides, scarlet-toes was Webster's sister, and she'd been in that hysterical state because her husband had just left her for a younger woman and their son was taking it badly. He was called Milton, the boy that is, after the town in which he'd been born, not the poet.

Harold was quiet after that, mute as the van advanced towards a smudge of mountains. Looking sideways at him, at the tuft of his beard, the brown spots sprinkling his podgy hands, the constant jiggling of his left knee, Rose was convinced he was a soul immersed in darkness. Perhaps that was why, like herself, he was anxious to find Dr Wheeler. Many years before, when she'd thought nothing could save her, Dr Wheeler had shown her the way. He'd never spelt anything out, never mentioned God, only nudged her towards the belief that redemption was necessary.

*   *   *

Wanakena was not far from Canada, if you were a bird. It was Red Indian country and originally settlers had come here to cut down trees and work in Benson's mine. Harold didn't know for sure what the mine had produced, although he thought

61

it might have been iron ore. Rose had heard of that at school, along with oxbow bends. There was a small village, a forest, a graveyard, a lake and a river. Some of the gardens blazed with sunflowers and there was a shop selling Indian relics. Harold said there was nothing of interest to be bought save pretend scalps and arrowheads.

His friend Mirabella lived in a one-storied timber house on stilts, wooden steps leading down to a patch of earth entirely surrounded by trees. She had to keep the lights on because the sun never got through the windows. She was middle-aged, handsome, and wore jodhpurs though she hadn't got a horse. When she spoke she sounded very confident, bossy, rather like Mrs Shaefer. Rose thought it was because American women weren't shy of appearing superior to men.

The rooms in the house were spacious, with vast fireplaces and a lot of oak furniture, yet Mirabella kept apologising for the lack of amenities. She explained she always came here at the beginning of June to escape the heat of her apartment in New York. 'You wouldn't believe,' she told Rose, 'how often I've been in danger of frying.'

Dr Wheeler wasn't there. Mirabella said that she hadn't set eyes on him for two years, but a letter had arrived a couple of days ago mentioning that he believed his friend Rose was in the States and that he could be contacted at an address in California.

Harold didn't seem surprised, didn't even ask to see the letter. He told Mirabella that Shaefer sent his love, then collapsed onto one of the many sofas. 'Oh yes,' he remembered, 'Jesse wanted me to remind you that you still have his poster of Lyndon Johnson dressed as a cowboy.'

62

Mirabella was very chatty. She talked about a Miss Durant and a Miss Jenks who had come from New York in 1910 and bought up ten houses, including the one they now sat in. Possibly, although in those days it had never been brought into the open, they had been more than just friends. There was a photograph of Miss Jenks above the main fireplace. She was very old, mouth a grim pencil line, and wore a man's cap on her head. Before her, a Madame Tweedy, a music teacher, had lived here scandalously with a lumberjack. When he died, mysteriously, from a gash in his throat, a girl had replaced him, one who looked so like a leopard, all spots and snarling teeth, that the villagers had run away screaming. 'I've a drawing somewhere,' Mirabella said and, jumping up, began rummaging in drawers.

'Could I see Dr Wheeler's letter?' Rose asked.

'Later, later,' Mirabella promised. Unable to find the drawing of the leopard girl she embarked on a story about a desolate family, the McDills, who had lived across the Oswegatchie River. 'They had four children,' she said, 'two girls and twin boys, one with red hair.'

'Did he say why he keeps moving?' said Rose.

'He was just a kid, no more than six years of age, but he apparently brought a dead wild-cat back to life, which ever after howled at the moon. It was claimed he was possessed by the devil. Ignorance, of course. The state took him away and his sisters became prostitutes.'

'I need to see it,' Rose said.

'Those days,' Mirabella declared, 'tragedy was in the air one breathed.'

'It is now,' Rose said. 'Nothing's changed.'

A meal was served when Harold woke up. It was pink lamb, not properly roasted, accompanied by a lot of green things. Harold said, 'Jesse rang you, I guess,' at which Mirabella nodded. The talk that followed was mostly about the Shaefers and how well Jesse and George were managing their lives, apart from the problem of their only child who was obviously heading for trouble.

'He stays out all night,' Mirabella said.

Harold said, 'You can hardly blame him.'

An hour passed before Rose felt able to bring up Dr Wheeler's letter again, by which time Harold had stumbled back to the sofa. Soon, judging by the snuffling noises emerging from the velvet cushions, he sank into the land of dreams.

'I'm sorry to be a nuisance,' Rose said, 'but I have to see that letter.'

It was very brief, merely an address in a town called Malibu to be given to Rose, and a polite hope that Mirabella was keeping well. He spelt Rose's name without a capital R.

'We had such good times in the old days,' Mirabella said. 'We all went to Paris once, at Fred's expense. Jesse . . . Bob Maitland . . . me.'

'When did Dr Wheeler leave?' Rose asked.

'Leave?' Mirabella looked puzzled.

'He said he'd be here,' Rose said. 'That's why I've come. I got a letter in Washington.'

Mirabella was forking the remains of lettuce leaves into a paper bag; one of her fingers was bound with sticking plaster. 'Why would he be here?' she queried. 'He's on the Kennedy campaign trail . . . somewhere in Oregon.'

'But he's dead,' said Rose.

Mirabella giggled. 'Not that one,' she corrected.

64

'His brother.'

It was evening when Harold woke. He scratched at his beard like a man infected with creepy crawlies and said he needed a walk. When Rose asked if she could come too, he flatly refused. 'You're not to go out,' he ordered.

'You'll be pleased with the rose bush,' Mirabella said. 'It's rambling towards heaven.'

She handed him a torch, in case it grew dark. Before he left he apologised for leaving her alone with Rose. 'You're to keep her inside,' he said. She said he was not to worry, message understood. Rose thought they were both rude.

When he'd gone, Mirabella asked how she and Harold had become acquainted. It was obvious from the gleam in her eyes that she took them to be more than just friends.

'We met through people I know . . . Polly and Bernard . . . a year or so ago. Bernard does business with a lot of Americans. I don't believe that Harold understands me, not really . . . we're not on the same wavelength . . . but he's been very kind and he paid for my aeroplane ticket. I don't have very much money myself, and it's lucky that he wants to find Dr Wheeler as much as I do. They go back a long way.'

'They do indeed,' Mirabella replied. She went to the stove and hovered there, fiddling with a jar of coffee. She was half smiling, as if remembering some joke.

'I knew Dr Wheeler when I was a child,' Rose said. 'He took an interest in me.'

'That's unique,' said Mirabella. 'Fred couldn't stand children.'

'He always told me that if ever I needed him,

65

he'd be waiting.'

'But not this time,' said Mirabella.

'I had a difficult childhood,' blurted Rose. 'I was saved by Dr Wheeler. He sorted me out.'

'Lucky you,' Mirabella said.

'Would you mind,' Rose asked, 'if I stretched my legs?' She was moving towards the door as she spoke.

'Best leave Harold alone,' Mirabella said. 'He's gone to look for his wife.'

Startled, Rose stared at her. 'His wife?' she repeated.

'Didn't he tell you?' Mirabella put aside the coffee jar and, taking Rose by the elbow, steered her to the table. She stood looking down at her, tugging at the plaster on her finger.

Rose said, 'He never mentioned he was married. Nobody did.'

'Men always keep things to themselves,' Mirabella told her. 'You shouldn't take it to heart.'

'I don't,' cried Rose. 'I just don't understand why he didn't tell me he was coming here to see his wife. Where is she?'

'Flat on her back,' Mirabella said, waving a damaged finger in the direction of the windows. 'Six foot under.'

The explanation that followed was brief and to the point. The wife, who was called Dollie, had fallen for another man. She had left Harold to be with him, but after twelve months he'd grown tired of her. She was an intelligent woman and should have known what she was getting herself into. 'It wasn't the first time she'd strayed,' Mirabella said, eyes glittering. 'She had a fling with Shaefer, but that was only sex.'

66

'Did Harold find out?'

'God, no. He thinks the world of Jesse. Anyway, Dollie came back to Wanakena and drowned in the lake beyond the trees. It was referred to as an accident, though some of the newspapers hinted at suicide. It was hushed up so that she could have a proper funeral. Suicides can't be put in consecrated ground.'

'Why here?' asked Rose.

'It's where they spent their honeymoon. I lent them the house.'

'I once told my teacher,' said Rose, 'that my mother had killed herself. It was a lie. I'd been off school for a week because of trouble at home and I sort of hinted that my mother had gone. Miss Albright took me into the staff room. I felt daft because outside the window Rita Dickens and her cronies in the fourth form were pulling out leaves they'd stuffed up their knickers . . . they were playing at having babies.'

'How inventive,' said Mirabella.

'I only meant Mother had gone away, but Miss Albright thought I meant really gone . . . gone for ever. Her eyes were all glittery.'

Mirabella was smiling again.

'I need to go outside,' Rose told her, 'to think things over. I promise I won't search for Harold.'

Once down the steps she was engulfed in shadows. It was as though she was small again, hurrying to meet Dr Wheeler in the green gloom. Ahead of her, patchy beneath the darkening heavens, she glimpsed the grey outline of that terrible lake.

Dr Wheeler was puffing on a cigarette. Gazing upwards, he said the smoke mingled with the presence

67

of those who had once lived. They were standing in front of the tombstone of Mary Eldridge, mother of two children, Ella and Robert, expired from fever, June 5th, 1868. She said she expected the children had cried a lot, even though Mrs Eldridge may not have been a good mother, at which he accused her of thinking of her own parents and always unkindly. None of us, he chided, can know how our actions affect other people, not until it's too late, nor blame others for our own mistakes.

The trees were so thick that the iron gate into the graveyard was partially hidden. Rose had difficulty in pushing it open. There was no church to be seen, simply row upon row of gravestones tilting forward on a march towards heaven. The racket of birds in the branches above was discordant enough to waken the dead.

She felt very sorry for Harold, and was vexed that she hadn't thought him capable either of being married or of suffering a tragedy. She'd always prided herself on being clever at sensing other people's emotions and the reasons for their deficiencies. It was curious, seeing that she had such a knowledge of character, that she hadn't divined Harold as being the sort of man to have a wife, let alone one who had topped herself.

She didn't stay long in the cemetery in case Harold appeared and got angry with her. If she had been in his shoes she wouldn't have liked to be followed. No wonder he had given her a funny look when she'd told him that story about Mother doing herself in. She went out of the gate, shoved it back into place and sat under the trees, watching the leaves blacken as the light leaked from the sky. She felt a mixture of sadness and elation; but then, other people's tragedies were always more affecting than one's own.

She was disturbed by a sudden noise, a sound halfway between a grunt and a roar, followed by a violent snapping of branches. In the distance a tiny beam of light, fluttery as a butterfly, skittered across the ground. She crouched down, waiting for the night to cease its quaking.

She was climbing the steps of the house when Washington Harold came up behind her. 'I've been searching for you,' he hissed. 'I told you not to go outside. You could have been killed.'

His face, illuminated by torchlight, was furrowed, angry.

'Killed?' she bleated.

Didn't she realise, he demanded, that there were bears nosing through the rubbish dump by the graveyard?

'Bears,' she said. 'Like the ones in the zoo?'

'Nothing like,' he retorted. 'These are on the loose, red in tooth and claw.'

If Harold was speaking the truth, it wasn't her he should have been yelling at. Mirabella hadn't mentioned a word about wild beasts, but then she was probably bored stiff and needed a spot of excitement. It couldn't be much fun, stuck in a forest where all the interesting events had happened a century ago.

'I'm sorry,' she lied, 'Mirabella warned me not to go outside, but I couldn't help myself.'

Harold calmed down when they got inside. He poured her a glass of wine and patted her hand as though he meant it; even so, she knew he didn't really see her. Nor did he bother to introduce her to the man in a knitted hat who was sitting beside

69

Mirabella at the table.

A minute after she had sat down she was aware of the man's bare foot rubbing up and down her leg. She didn't mind, it being something she was used to, and besides, he was very generous in handing out cigarettes. He had bushy eyebrows and a scar on his upper lip. Now and then Mirabella glanced at her, expression wary; the confident woman had gone.

There was a lot of talk about the disaster of the Vietnam war and how the sooner they got shut of President Johnson the better it would be for everyone. Harold wanted Richard Nixon to win because he came from a Quaker background, one far removed from the established aristocrats of New England or the landowners of the South. He'd emerged, Harold said, from stock that had fought and prayed their way across a continent.

A picture came into Rose's head of a horde of Red Indians galloping down a mountain towards a clearing filled with people on their knees.

The man in the hat—he had the curious name of Dear Heart—wasn't in favour of Nixon, even though he apparently worked in the same law firm on Wall Street. Mirabella was of the opinion that Mr Kennedy would beat someone called McCarthy when it came to the California primary. 'He's got to,' she said. 'For all our sakes.'

'Don't bet on it,' the hat-man shouted.

'Do you remember that film?' Rose interrupted, looking at Harold, 'with that little boy crouching beside his dead mother? She'd been tomahawked. There was a lot of blood.'

'He may win, but he won't live long enough to take it any further,' the hat-man said. 'The Cubans have it in for him. It's tit for tat after what he tried to do to Castro. Think what happened in Los Angeles last month . . .'

Neither Harold nor Mirabella seemed to know what he was talking about.

'He was shot at when he left that college in the San Fernando valley.'

'It was a stone-throwing, not a shooting,' Harold argued. 'Someone tossed a brick from a bridge. He just had a bruise on his cheek.'

'The British news said it was a gunshot,' Dear Heart said, 'and British news is always accurate.' Rose clapped her hands, but nobody joined in.

Later, Harold abandoned his plan of returning to the van and said he'd sleep on the sofa. He could have had a bedroom but insisted he needed to listen out for anyone roaming about outside. Rose didn't think he was worried about bears; for a moment it crossed her mind that he was thinking of Red Indians, but she had drunk too much to be afraid. The man in the hat said he'd occupy the other couch, in case of trouble, but she saw the look he gave Mirabella.

She was taken to a room with a photograph on the wall of a woman surrounded by nine children. Rose counted them. Their mother was quite young and obviously as poor as a church mouse. Mirabella, eyes outlined in black pencil, said the woman's name was Ethel. Indicating the basin and the switch on the bedside lamp, she fled.

Rose would have liked to have a chat, woman to woman. It was odd that someone so good at applying make-up should be so averse to talking face to face.

71

CHAPTER SEVEN

Before Harold went to bed he asked Mirabella if it was all right for him to stay longer, not another night, but maybe most of the following day. It was good to be with her, he stressed, and to renew ties with Gerhardt, but more importantly the rose bush above Dollie's grave needed pruning. He said, voice jagged, 'It's overgrown . . . only to be expected.'

She told him he could stay as long as he wanted, that, in the circumstances, she needed him. He knew what she meant. She was mad about Gerhardt Kelmann but it wasn't a happy union—he was giving her grief.

When he woke it was no surprise to find that Kelmann wasn't on the couch by the fireplace, just his hat and his trousers in a heap against the woodpile. After downing a glass of milk, he took a carving knife from the kitchen drawer and stepped out into the forest. He inspected the camper, which was parked in a clearing round the side of the house, and was irritated at the bird droppings splattered on its hood. Kelmann's car and Mirabella's were untouched.

The bush above Dollie's grave had spiralled out of control. There were flowers, lemon yellow, thrusting up among the dead and dying blooms; the fierce thorns tore at the skin on his arms.

An hour or so passed, and then, breathless, he stretched out on the colourless grass. Try as he might, he couldn't see Dollie's face. Once, the month before she had left him for Wheeler, she'd said that time would make him forget her, that she would fade like paintwork. 'Paintwork,' he'd shouted, 'can last a lifetime.' He'd cease to think of her, she insisted, because he was the innocent party; she, the betrayer, would remember him for ever. He reckoned it was a spurious argument.

'There you are,' boomed a voice; Gerhardt Kelmann thudded down beside him. 'If I'm in the way,' he said, 'just tell me to get lost.'

He didn't know Kelmann well, but he knew he'd suffered more grievously than himself. A child's exposure to sudden death was surely more shocking than that experienced by an adult. When Kelmann was eleven years old, he had found his father, a roofing contractor, head stoved in, sprawled on a pathway leading to the Long Island Railway. Nobody had been charged, nobody punished, but then neither had the person responsible for Dollie's end. Not yet.

'The worst thing,' he said, sitting up and kicking at the soil around the grave, 'is to realise that time blocks out most things.'

'It has to,' Kelmann said, 'otherwise we'd go mad.'

The sun was now very strong, piercing fire through the lacework of leaves. Kelmann lit a cigarette. Puffing out smoke, he said, 'She's a strange girl.'

Harold nodded. He knew who he meant.

'She only talks about college days.'

'Yes,' he said. 'I guess so.'

'Do you know why?'

'It's not my concern.'

They both fell silent. Harold rubbed his thumb back and forward across the swollen mosquito bite on his cheek. No longer an irritant, it was still part

73

of him.

Kelmann said, 'She told me you're both looking for Fred Wheeler.'

'She is,' he replied, 'I'm just the driver.' He knelt and stuck the knife into the earth that held his skeleton of love; the metal handle quivered upright, flashing silver. 'I need to be alone,' he told Kelmann, and strode away in the direction of the lake.

Returning to the house an hour later, he attended to his scratched arms. He used a towel in the bathroom to mop away the blood. When he went through into the living room, Mirabella was alone. She said that Gerhardt and Rose had gone into the village to look at Indian artefacts, that his girlfriend was after scalps, Gerhardt's among them. Hadn't he noticed how she'd snuggled up to him?

'She's not my girl,' he protested. 'And Rose isn't interested in men, just Wheeler. She lives in the past.'

'Who doesn't?' Mirabella moaned, black tears dripping from her pencilled eyes. Unable to keep still, she restlessly stalked the room, fiddling with the ornaments on the mantelshelf, smoothing the cloth on the table, clicking the radio switch on and off.

'For God's sake sit down,' he bellowed, and she did, collapsing onto the sofa, face pressed against a velvet cushion, sobs wobbling her shoulders.

After a moment he crouched beside her, hand patting her head. 'You've always known it wasn't going to work,' he soothed. 'Kelmann isn't the sort of guy to confine himself to one woman . . . you told me that yourself.'

'Knowing and hoping are two different things,'

74

she said, voice smothered. 'You of all people should understand that.'

'In my case,' he reminded her, 'hope has long since gone underground.'

She sat up at that, wiping her face with the back of her hand. 'I'm just tired,' she murmured, and allowed him to hug her.

They were still in that position, her head on his breast and his mouth against her hair, when Rose and Kelmann came back. Rose was holding a mess of goldenrod. 'These flowers are for you,' she said, thrusting them towards Mirabella.

'They're wild,' Harold said. 'They'll be dead in an hour.' He released his hold and stood up, indicating that Kelmann should take his place. Kelmann grinned, and remained standing.

'We met a man,' Rose burbled, 'who was a direct descendant of a Red Indian called Little Bush Fire. He had a prominent nose, a bit like mine. He said he wouldn't be at all surprised if we didn't come from the same ancestors.' Still clutching her bunch of goldenrod, she ran to the fireplace and on tiptoe studied her face in the glass above.

'It's a special day,' Kelmann said, addressing Mirabella. 'Some kind of a remembrance of an incident two hundred years ago.'

'Is that so?' she responded. 'I couldn't care less.'

'A British colonel arrived here and made friends with an Indian chief.'

'How interesting,' she said, voice heavy with sarcasm. She was looking at him as though he'd crawled out from under a stone.

'After a few trinkets changed hands, the chief said it was all right for the settlers to move in. He even promised to supply timber for shacks.'

'That was nice, wasn't it?' Rose said. 'Really nice.'

'Trouble was,' continued Kelmann, 'these so-called settlers were the crazed occupants of English prisons . . . the mad and the bad.'

Mirabella was crying again, cushion clutched to her mouth.

'It's important to make allowances,' Rose said. She turned to face Kelmann, one finger tracing the outline of her nose. 'They were probably all over the shop due to their upbringing.'

'To hell with that,' he thundered. 'They came here, slaughtered the inhabitants, then made a fortune out of mining.'

Rose gazed at him, eyes startled. Then she moved to the open door and stood there, shoulders hunched. Harold followed her.

'I'm all right,' she whispered. 'Really I am.'

'It's not you I'm concerned about,' he hissed, nudging her down the steps and striding into the trees.

Some distance from the churchyard, he confronted her. He told her she shouldn't have gone off with Kelmann. Didn't she realise that Mirabella needed to talk to him?

'But it was Mirabella who told us to go,' Rose said.

'Didn't you notice how hurt she was?'

'It's not him that's making her cry,' she shouted. 'She doesn't give a fig about him.'

He stared at her. She was brushing the leaves of those wild flowers against her cheek and for the first time he registered the colour of her eyes.

She said, 'I don't know what's really wrong with her, but it happened a long time ago. What was she

76

like way back?'

'I don't want to talk about it,' he said. 'I've other things on my mind.'

It was then that she asked him why he hadn't told her about his wife. He insisted that it was a private matter. He was astonished at the way she had turned the conversation away from herself. He said, 'Your eyes . . . they're green.'

She was smiling. 'You haven't seen me before now,' she said, 'not properly. That's why you keep snubbing me. Americans never tell the truth . . . I don't mean you lie, more that you find it easier to hide things. Where I come from we let everything out.'

He showed her Dollie's grave. She didn't say much, just that the roses looked chastened. Then she said she was worried about getting to that place where Dr Wheeler was staying. She had to get back to England quite soon or she'd lose her job.

Kelmann had gone when they returned to the house. Mirabella was holding a towel to her lips. It was the same one Harold had used on his torn arms. She said that Kelmann had punched her before he left. She was quite calm and although her cheeks were flushed, her mouth didn't appear swollen.

She kissed Rose goodbye and said she was sorry to see her leave. As they bumped from the narrow path onto the highway, Kelmann's car approached from the opposite direction.

'Harold, stop . . .' Rose cried, but he didn't. He had enough problems of his own.

CHAPTER EIGHT

They were two hundred and fifty miles from Wanakena, speeding under darkening skies along a winding road somewhere near Lake Erie, when for the umpteenth time Harold said he needed to pee. Clutching his parts he ran into a scattering of trees. The word he actually used was urinate, which Rose found offensive.

He left the door open; she lit a cigarette and moved into his seat so that he wouldn't complain about the smell of tobacco. She was puffing away, legs dangling above the grass verge, when suddenly she was confronted by a man wearing a soutane. He was brandishing a prayer book with a picture of the Virgin Mary on the cover. 'Praise be,' he wheezed, 'my car's broken down,' and he jabbed a finger at the road behind. Before she could reply he ran round the side of the van, opened the door and climbed in. 'Drive,' he ordered. 'People are depending on me.' At that moment Harold emerged from the trees.

The man's name was Monsignor Secker. When his car had gone wrong he'd been on his way to conduct a Mass for the Dead, that of a young soldier whose body had been flown home from Saigon and buried in a hurry. The boy's mother had fortunately been dissuaded from looking inside the coffin; it wouldn't have been a pleasant sight.

'Couldn't he have been covered with a flag,' Rose asked, 'and flowers laid over his face?'

Monsignor Secker said, 'He didn't have one.'

Harold murmured, 'This damned war,' and

would have added more if the priest hadn't kept telling him to drive faster. Rose was jammed between the two of them, her cigarette still burning. There was no way of stubbing it out and she didn't dare toss it out of the window in case it caused a fire.

She was thinking of the boy's mother and the things that would have to be done, now that her child was deep in the ground. There'd be his photograph, in uniform, to be hung on the wall, the gathering together of letters and school reports, the folding up of clothes in the wardrobe; they wouldn't be given away, not for a year or so, not until the moths had done their worst. Some days, the family dog would be held close for the mother to whisper in its ear that its childhood friend was never coming back. The images in Rose's mind were so clear— the dog's ears erect, quivering—that tears stung her eyes.

She was squashing along the windy shore, the breaking waves spitting water on her shoes. She'd been moaning that she couldn't bear the way Father constantly raged at Mother, the dirty names he called her. It tore her heart. Dr Wheeler said a certain amount of pain or trouble was necessary at all times. A ship without ballast was unstable, not able to sail straight. There was no greater absurdity than the belief that the enormous amount of pain in the world served no purpose. Unless one accepted that suffering was the direct and immediate object of life, existence was futile. In any case, the longer one lived the more clearly one realised that life was a cheat, a disappointment. All the same, above the hissing of the sea, he'd begun to hum that optimistic song about bluebirds flying over the white cliffs of Dover.

The church was in a place called Salamanca, which was off Harold's route, a fact he mentioned quite loudly. The Monsignor was too busy shouting out directions to take any notice. When they arrived on the outskirts of a sprawl of industrial buildings, he thumped his knee with relief. Rose could tell by the state of the paint-peeling one-storey wooden houses and the amount of rubbish in the gutters that it wasn't a town with money. Driving down a side street they passed the lit windows of a shop advertising the selling of oysters, a trestle table piled with potatoes and a store with electrical goods heaped outside. A skinny goat tethered to a post was headbutting a bucket. The priest said this had once been Iroquois Indian territory but now it was home to railroad workers. His own father had worked as a maintenance man on the Rochester to Buffalo railroad.

'Turn left,' he ordered. A solitary street lamp illuminated the front of a stone church with a statue of Jesus, hands outstretched, on a plinth in the porch. Beyond, beneath black clouds, was the unexpected fuzz of an orchard in bloom.

Three people were waiting on the church path: a stout woman in a long black skirt, an elderly man in a broad-brimmed hat and a young girl teetering on high heels. When the priest leapt out of the van, the fat woman waved her arms about and tottered towards him.

Rose said, 'I've never been to an American funeral. Do you think I could join them, just for five minutes? It would be something to tell Polly and Bernard.' She didn't expect Harold to agree, but he nodded. He needed to buy provisions. She wasn't to be too long, seeing the skies were about to open and they ought to be looking for a campsite. He wouldn't be surprised if the weather turned real bad.

The Mass had already begun when she entered the porch. She could hear the murmur of the congregation repeatedly begging Christ to have mercy on them. She took some time smoothing her hair and buttoning up her raincoat, and when she pushed open the door the Monsignor was asking the Lord to release the soul of the departed from the bonds of sin. *May he escape the sentence of condemnation and enjoy the bliss of eternal light.*

There were no more than twenty people in the pews; she needn't have worried about her appearance, for apart from the old man in the large hat, no one was appropriately dressed. Most of the men were clad in overalls and two of the women wore fur coats that had seen better days.

It was a modest interior, with dim Stations of the Cross on either wall, candles guttering on the altar, and a statue of the Virgin Mary beneath the pulpit. The air was stifling and only a thin gleam of light penetrated the stained glass of the windows.

She moved as close to the front as she dared and knelt on a threadbare silk cushion. The priest began to recite from the Sequence for the Dead. *Judex ergo cum sedebit, quidquid latet apparebit: nil inultum remanebit . . . Juste judex ultionis, donum fac remissionis.* Though she'd learnt Latin at school, and been quite good at it, she understood but two lines: *Whatever is hidden will be seen, nothing will remain unpunished.*

She supposed the woman seated nearest to the altar, grey wisps of hair straggling her bent neck, must be the bereft mother, though there was no

81

trembling of the shoulders, no sound of subdued weeping. Maybe it was difficult to produce tears when there wasn't a coffin to prod the emotions.

It was funny, Rose thought, how immediately she had once embraced the Catholic faith, and how easily she had walked away. She'd become a convert when she was sixteen, after Mother had given the baby up for adoption. She'd run off to Scotland and worked in a pub, and at Easter, Jeffrey Crouch, the landlord, had taken her to a midnight Mass. At some point a row of candles had been snuffed out, one by one. Each time the flame died, she had to strike her breast and shout, *Through my fault, my fault, my most grievous fault*, until she was drowned in incense-filled darkness. It was exhilarating, addictive. If she'd been in England she wouldn't have been allowed to change her religion, not under the age of twenty-one, because it was illegal without parental consent. It was different in Scotland. She'd been sent to a convent for instruction and would have enjoyed arguing about what the love of God really amounted to—if the nun in charge hadn't been incarcerated since she was twelve years old. It wouldn't have been nice to express doubts to someone so absent from the world.

It was the Beatles, she reflected, and the hydrogen bomb . . . and people taking drugs— something she'd never done—that had made faith dry up.

She'd never confided in Dr Wheeler, either about her conversion or the baby. She hadn't seen him for four years and by the time they met again, that last time at Charing Cross station, belief had long since dribbled away and he was off to America.

She was still on her knees when the mourners

shuffled down the aisle. The mother with the grey hair wore a faded pink dress; as though tasting death, her tongue flicked her lips. Rose pretended she was praying, keeping her clasped fingers close to her face in case they were all looking at her.

She remained crouching there until she heard the blasting of a horn. It was typical of Harold to be disrespectful. When she climbed in beside him he apologised for making such a row. 'I didn't want that priest guy asking for a lift back to his car,' he explained.

'He'll be too busy comforting the boy's mother,' she said. 'And I expect there'll be refreshments.'

'By the look of her,' he replied, indicating the fat woman in the black skirt propped against the nailed feet of Jesus, 'she's been refreshing herself all day.'

She didn't see the point in telling him he'd got the wrong woman.

He was tardy in starting the engine, and the next moment Monsignor Secker was running towards them. Reluctantly, Harold waited. He needn't have worried, the priest only wanted to thank him. The local priest had offered him a bed for the night and a breakdown truck was already on its way to fetch his car.

Rose said, 'Do tell the mum how sorry I am for her loss.'

The Monsignor said such sentiments were much appreciated but the mother wasn't present. She'd been taken to hospital earlier that morning. A stroke, he believed.

'God Almighty,' Harold murmured, and wound up the window.

*   *   *

Rain started to fall as they rejoined the highway they'd abandoned earlier. The sky now hung metallic grey and torrents of water buffeted the insect-smeared windscreen. Harold said the radio had given warning of a tornado. 'How exciting,' she trilled, at which he called her a fool. If they didn't find a campsite quite soon they'd need to spend the night in a motel; he was worried about the stuff on the roof.

Under the ridge of a pass, he stopped to buy gasoline. Nearby, a row of cabins stood next to a café dominated by a sign printed with the words, *No cheques cashed unless accompanied by fingerprints.*

'It's a joke, isn't it?' she queried.

'Not entirely,' he said, and ordered her to follow him.

The café was deserted save for a young man in charge of the desk. He had a hairstyle like Elvis Presley's. Rose felt he was wasted in his position, mostly because his eyes sparkled with hope. When he took down the keys from the board behind him and swaggered out to show them a room, she was dazzled by his two-tone shoes. Harold asked if there was somewhere under cover where he could park the camper, preferably a lock-up.

'There's a shed with a tin roof,' Elvis told him. 'But it don't have no doors.'

The cabin was primitive, just one room with a bed, a row of hooks on the back of the door, a one-legged stool and a chamberpot in the corner. There was no washbasin and the counterpane had a large stain near the pillows. According to Harold the air smelt funny, a mixture of dampness and fried food. Suddenly he announced he'd best stay in the camper, to keep an eye on his belongings. She could have the room. What with the rain and no security he'd have to keep the door locked and she wouldn't like that, would she?

'No, I wouldn't,' she agreed. 'I'd get claustrophobia.' It was a good excuse, one that would save her from his nightly nagging to wash her face and scrub her teeth. 'But,' she added, 'I don't want to cause you expense.'

'It's only two dollars. And by the look of the place that's a dollar too much.'

She didn't turn the light off and got into bed in her clothes. Presently she was aware of a dripping sound. Rain was coming through the ceiling, drop by drop, plopping into the chamberpot. She remembered Auntie Phyllis used to have such a receptacle, its china bowl decorated with red roses. The lav was in the back yard. Father had boasted, mouth grim, that he'd gained his education from a childhood spent reading old newspapers while waiting to evacuate.

She tried to think of the boy without a face and of his stricken mother, but all she could see in her head was Auntie Phyllis squatting on the potty, nightie hauled up above her backside, the street lamp glittering off the curlers in her hair.

CHAPTER NINE

At six o'clock the following morning, Harold knocked on Rose's door and shouted that she should join him in the restaurant. He had endured a disturbed night spent clambering in and out of

85

the camper, convinced he'd heard scraping noises and stealthy footsteps. Emerging from the black confines of the tin shack, he had done sentry duty beneath a canopy of stars.

When Rose appeared she was dressed in her usual outfit of trousers and raincoat, even though the rain had ceased and the sun was climbing into a cloudless sky. In the middle of chewing on her one slice of toast, she offered him some English shillings in exchange for a dollar. He gave her what she needed, but refused the coins spilled onto the table.

'What are you going to buy?' he asked, at which she muttered something about it being women's stuff, which was a lie because she went straight to the tobacco counter. When she'd paid for what she'd bought she called to him that she was going out for a spot of fresh air. He assumed she wanted a cigarette and wondered why she preferred to smoke on her own.

As they drove out of Pennsylvania into Ohio she chirruped that it must be like crossing from Lancashire into Yorkshire. When told they were halfway to Chicago, she sat up and even began to study the map, but after no more than a moment cast it aside and announced that she knew about Chicago from gangster pictures. 'It's where,' she said, 'Al Capone did all his killing.'

Approaching Cleveland, he was seized with a desire to visit his old university and made the detour to Akron. He wasn't sure it was a good idea, but something compelled him. A queer sense of loneliness filled his being, an isolation of the spirit. He reasoned it had to do with lack of sleep, that and the turmoil of his thoughts.

When they reached the campus he ordered Rose to stay where she was. She pulled a face, but he took no notice. Her presence was unsettling. She was too confrontational, too apt to speak without thinking. For more than two hours she had talked about nothing but the Holy Spirit and the Day of Wrath. The funeral had brought out the worst in her. She reckoned even the dead soldier would face the flames of everlasting hell. He was beginning to believe that some power, God even, had joined them together in order to crush his resolution.

Shoulders bowed, he trudged towards the administration buildings. There was no one about save for an old man with a wart on his nose, sitting on a chair outside the closed doors. He asked Harold his business.

'Class of 1945,' he volunteered. 'I remember you, but I don't expect you remember me . . . too many faces.' He didn't explain it was the wart that he found memorable.

'Nope, I don't,' the old man replied, 'but that ain't surprising. Most days I don't recall me own name.'

The gymnasium lay behind the chemistry lab. He had a need to go there and stare through the windows. He had not been altogether happy during those long-gone years—no surprise there—but at least he had partially got away from the suffocating presence of his mother. Memories swirled through his head like a flock of birds: that first encounter in the locker room with a young Shaefer, watery-eyed at the news that Mahatma Gandhi had been shot; the fist fight with Meredith Manning, caught stoning Mrs Arlington's cat; his first glorious lapse into drunkenness when the music of the dance band

87

had drowned his shyness and Shaefer, a guiding arm about his shoulders, had walked him into the moonlight. Shaefer was his true friend, one who never had nor ever would betray him. Lastly, vivid, an image of his mother advancing towards the Rothschild Building, arm in a sling of black silk dotted with fake diamonds. His second stepfather had pushed her to the floor after receiving a hefty bill for two bronze horses she'd had installed on the gates of their house on Long Island, copies of those she'd seen on St Mark's Basilica in Venice. Her arm hadn't suffered lasting damage, but she had never been shy of attracting attention. Only Shaefer had understood that Harold's misery stemmed from embarrassment rather than pity.

The interior of the gym had altered. The vaulting box was no longer there, nor the row of lockers where once his name had been displayed; gone from the walls the photographs of the baseball teams, gone the yellow ropes that used to dangle from hooks in the ceiling. Time, he thought, was fast wiping out his life.

Rose was sitting outside on the grass when he returned, rubbing the dirt from between her toes. He asked if she was hungry, and as always she said she wasn't. When she sat beside him in the camper, he was aware she was staring at him.

She said, 'Your face looks funny.'

'So I've been told,' he quipped.

'It never does any good,' she said, 'to dwell on things that can't be changed . . . that way madness lies.'

It was curious, he thought, how sometimes she appeared educated. Glancing sideways at her, he recognised the expression on her face, a mixture of unease and fortitude. She was trying hard, he reckoned, to make the best of a disappointing situation. Taking stock of his behaviour, his lack of sympathy, the absence of interest in his voice whenever she waxed on about her childhood, he resolved to make amends. God knows, he knew better than most what it was like to feel undervalued.

'Would you,' he asked suddenly, 'like to go to a movie?'

'Yes,' she said, eyes shining, 'but only if you would.' She was happy now.

He made for Cedar Point and a campsite on a hillside. It was well equipped, boasting a miniature golf course and a large swimming pool, its blue waters mirroring the sky. Beyond, below the campers and the tents, a jumble of fishing boats jostled the dazzling curve of Lake Erie.

Rose was impressed. She stared at the men in shorts and the plump women lounging on chairs, but turned away from the screaming children running and tumbling beneath the cedar trees. Nearby, a baby strapped into a high chair was banging its wooden tray with a spoon; he noticed that Rose winced at the sound and immediately put on her sunglasses. He had the notion that it wasn't just the sun she was blotting out.

Although he was hungry, he thought it best to see to cleanliness first. Indicating the laundry room beside the store, he asked Rose if she had any clothes that needed washing. 'No,' she said. 'Too much cleaning makes us susceptible to germs.' A superior smile on her face, she watched as he stripped the mattress of its covering and beat the pillows against the trunk of a tree. 'Insects will wriggle in,' she warned. Then she wandered off, which annoyed him because he could have done with some help.

When he came back from the laundry room she was squatting on the grass some distance from the camper, close to an elderly man in a straw hat. They weren't talking to each other. He was slumped in an armchair and Rose was rocking backwards and forwards, eyes to the ground. Then a younger man appeared and said something to her, at which she got up and engaged him in conversation. She appeared animated and did most of the talking. Once, she held up her hand and wafted it in front of the man's face, as if wiping out something she didn't want to hear.

Later, Harold asked her about the old boy in the chair.

She said, 'His name's Theodore. He once lived in England.'

'I guess,' he said, thinking of the man's age, 'that he talked a lot of moonshine.'

'No,' she corrected, 'as a matter of fact he talked perfect sense. He said he was rotting.'

'Rotting . . .?'

'Hearing, innards, feet, eyesight, bones . . . nothing as it used to be.'

'Jesus,' he said. 'Obviously not a cheerful guy.'

'He hadn't expected to be cheerful,' she said, 'not once he got old. He's just facing life as it's meant to be. He always knew he would rot.'

'Jesus,' he said again, and told her to get into the camper.

The cinema screen was in a field alongside the golf course. Rose was amazed that films could be shown in the open air. The movie was called

The Third Man and was about an American guy arriving in Vienna to stay with his best friend, only the friend turned out to be dead, though not for long. Orson Welles played the elusive character and ended up running through the sewers. Harold had seen it before and dozed intermittently. Rose thought the film wonderful, but couldn't understand why the Yank wanted to kill Orson Welles. She said it didn't make sense, a man endlessly looking for his friend, and then shooting him when he found him. It wasn't normal. And she only remembered two men. Who was the third? Harold tried to explain that the Welles character was bad and that he deserved to die, but she argued that no real friendship could ever end in that sort of way, no matter what the circumstances. In the end he gave up and agreed with her, to keep her quiet.

Before she went to bed she asked to borrow a piece of paper and something to write with. Her father's pen had gone missing. He could hear the rumblings of her stomach as she scribbled. He'd eaten half a chicken, she no more than a mouthful of bread. He was surprised she wasn't turning into a skeleton, like someone else he knew. When she climbed into the camper she left the bit of paper by the fire. To his astonishment, she had written something in Latin, albeit badly spelt. *Recordez Jesus pie, quod sum cause tua via, ne me perder illa die.* With difficulty he deciphered the words: *Remember gracious Jesus, that I am the cause of your journey, do not let me be lost on that day.*

Yet again he slept badly, waking from a dream of walking with Wheeler through a field of maize. He'd been blinded by the sun blazing on Wheeler's hair, that and the blue vein pulsing on his forehead.

91

They'd had a conversation, an important one, but he couldn't remember what it was about.

*   *   *

The next afternoon, approaching Chicago, he gave Rose a lecture on the city to shut her up; she was still meandering on about God. Originally, he told her, it had been known as Fort Dearborn, a settlement on the shores of Lake Michigan with no more than a hundred inhabitants. Sixty years later, renamed, it housed over a million and had become the largest grain market in the world.

She didn't seem interested. He stopped himself from telling her that the downtown area had been burnt to the ground in 1871. It would only have started her off again on the fires of hell. Then she asked what grain was. He laughed and didn't reply, convinced she was joking.

Without thinking, he came to a halt in a street in Wicker Park, a suburb of the city and once a neighbourhood of the rich. The great houses had long since multiplied into apartments, the lawns into storage spaces for trashcans and automobiles. Rose, remembering the address on the letter, asked him to show her the place where Wheeler had stayed some weeks ago.

'It's a waste of time,' he argued. 'He's long gone.'

'I just need to see it.'

'What's the point?'

'You needn't come,' she snapped. 'Just tell me where to go.'

Frowning, he indicated a house further down the street, its white tower stabbing the cobalt sky. She was opening the door when a wave of sound followed by a thunderous roar swept the air. The camper shook. Startled, she turned and clutched his arm. 'It's the El,' he reassured her, 'just a train,' and pointed at the track running level with the chimney pots.

'No wonder he chose to stay here,' she said. 'He and his wife used to live next door to a railway crossing . . . and his house had a tower as well.'

'Wheeler didn't have a wife.'

'Yes he did . . . she rode a bike. She always pushed in front of me in the chip shop.'

'What did she look like?' he demanded, convinced she was lying.

'Old, plump, lots of grey curls under a straw hat.'

'He never mentioned he was married.'

'Neither did you,' she retorted, which rendered him silent.

He was getting short of money and needed to cash a cheque. She insisted on coming with him. 'I could do with the exercise,' she said. 'My bottom's gone numb.'

He'd wanted her to stand guard over the camper, but she was already leaping out of the door. Whatever store they passed she darted away to look in the windows. She couldn't keep her thoughts to herself, letting loose little screams of astonishment as she swivelled round to scrutinise the people streaming along the sidewalk, making remarks in a loud voice as to the mixture of races. 'That coloured man,' she shouted, nudging him in the ribs, 'had Chinese eyes.' He wished her dead.

The bank was only half full and he didn't have long to wait. There was a limping woman ahead of him, and a second female at the adjacent grille, wearing a pink bow atop a beehive of dyed hair. He

93

was writing out a cheque when someone screamed. He turned to see a man with a mask over his face holding Rose by the throat, a gun to her temple. She twisted round in his arm and buried her face in his coat; taken aback, he patted her head as though comforting a puppy. A man by the entrance, a scarf covering his nose and mouth, ordered everyone to fall to the floor.

The next few seconds were confused, traumatic. Some part of Harold contemplated jumping to his feet and wrestling Rose from the gunman, but a larger part kept him on his stomach, face to the wooden floor, heart pounding. Minutes later, although it might have been hours, a stampede of armed police entered the building, followed by the gunman and his accomplice being overpowered. No shots were fired. The man holding Rose threw his weapon to the floor. When the mask was torn from his face his expression was puzzled. Trembling, Harold felt he had taken part in a movie. Aghast, he discovered he'd wet himself.

Rose and he were detained for questioning. He said he remembered nothing beyond the sound of his friend screaming.

'I didn't scream,' Rose protested. 'Why would I scream? I didn't think it was a real gun.'

He could tell the cops found her odd, partly on account of her English accent—that and her lack of hysteria. She said it was the woman with the pearl earrings and the bow in her hair who had screamed.

He said, 'I didn't notice the earrings.'

'I closed my eyes,' she told them. 'I've read about this sort of thing. They won't shoot you if you don't stare at their faces.'

She described a woman with a plaster on her

94

knee who had reached the counter seconds before Harold. There was also a man in the line behind, scribbling doodles on a newspaper, who was carrying a scarf before he raced for the doors and clamped it over his face.

'His scarf,' she said, 'was a tartan one . . . from Scotland. I don't know which clan.'

Asked where she would be staying, she said, 'It's somewhere in Malibu. A rich place by the sea.'

After studying his bank account details and accompanying them to the camper to examine Rose's passport and visa, the police allowed them to continue their journey.

Back on the road, Harold tried to talk to her. He was convinced she must feel fragile, frightened. He was appalled at his previous wish that she should die, tormented by the ludicrous thought that God had heard him.

'You can break down now,' he said. 'I'll understand. It's only normal after what you've been through.'

'I don't feel like breaking,' she said. 'It wasn't that out of the ordinary.'

He couldn't fathom her and decided that his own reaction had stemmed from an acute awareness of danger; certain people were more sensitive than others. To blot out the doubts crowding his mind, he turned on the radio in the middle of a political debate, about Kennedy's chances of winning the Oregon primary.

There is a feeling among ordinary Americans that there's a malfunction in society, one so gross and puzzling that no ordinary politician can bring relief . . . Kennedy alone can exert authority, charismatic authority . . .

But everyone knows charisma is unstable. It can prove intolerant, inflexible. Mistakes could be made . . . and the magic cloak, once ripped, can never be mended . . .

'I once had a cloak,' Rose gabbled. 'It was my auntie's. It's not true they can't be mended, not if you take them to a dressmaker.'

Irritated, he asked, 'Are you sure you didn't feel fear?'

'No,' she said. 'I'd read a book about it.'

'About what? By who?'

She said, 'I don't remember. Napoleon the first had something to with it, or the second. Dr Wheeler gave it to me.' Sliding down in her seat, she closed her eyes and blocked him out.

CHAPTER TEN

The nearer the van took Rose towards Los Angeles—the dream-like passages over hills dotted with juniper trees, the descents into swathes of sea-green lowlands, the tunnelling through black forests bordering deserted roads—the more elusive Dr Wheeler became. It was disconcerting. Sometimes, when there was nothing on either side of the track other than jagged rocks sloping down to distant valleys speckled with toy cows, he vanished altogether. Perplexed, she took out a photograph of him, the one she'd snapped at Charing Cross station, hand raised to obscure his face, wrist encased in the crocodile-skin strap of his watch.

'We'll find him,' Harold said. 'You mustn't worry.' He sounded kind, really understanding.

That night they stayed somewhere in a region called the Bad Lands, where, as the sun began to drop, the fiery hills and cliffs stopped blazing, fading pale rose and gold. The flies were particularly fierce and Harold spent the night squirting the inside of the van with a fog of insect repellent. In the end, Rose clambered out to seek sleep under a heaven hazy with starlight.

She was trying to work out what she would tell Polly and Bernard on her return. She would have to keep to herself what she felt about Harold, because he was their friend. He had, in fact, had a long discussion with her the day after the incident with the gunman, to do with his behaviour towards her, his lack of patience. It was due, he'd said, to his foolish expectations of what it might have been like—the two of them seeing such wonders of nature together—and his reaction to the way things had actually been between them. He was sorry, he said, if he'd been difficult, but she ought to understand that he wasn't used to spending time with a woman, not since the loss of his wife. It was clever, Rose thought, the way he shifted blame away from himself.

She'd nodded and said she quite understood, although if the truth be told she hadn't found him difficult, or rather she was so used to his sort of response that it hadn't bothered her. She didn't mind how he treated her, just as long as he got her to Dr Wheeler. His attitude was no different from that of her parents. He was unsure of who he was, frightened of who he might be. He rambled on a lot about being open with her, but he hadn't mentioned a word about weeing in his pants at the bank.

Harold stopped in a town near Yellowstone Park, anxious to make a telephone call about his investments. Above the drugstore in the dusty main street hung a tattered cutout of Santa Claus, sitting in his wagon without any reindeers. Americans, Rose thought, were very keen on Christmas. The men on the sidewalk were dressed like cowboys and most of the ladies tapped by in white high-heeled shoes. Behind a shop labelled 'Happy Hunting', a giant blue globe perched on stilts reared up towards the sky. Harold said it was a water tower.

He sent her into the post office to buy stamps while he went to make his call. There was a Wanted poster of James Earl Ray, killer of Martin Luther King Jr, on the main wall. Stuck there, it was much more startling than the image that flicked on and off on television screens. Plucking up courage, Rose asked the man behind the counter if she could have it. It would make a nice present for Polly and Bernard.

'In my country,' she explained, 'all of us are very anxious that Mr Ray should be brought to justice. I'll display it inside the House of Commons.'

It took time for her request to be understood—they thought she was a foreigner—but after she'd told them she was a close relation of the Prime Minister of England, permission was granted and she walked out with the poster rolled up under her arm.

They entered Yellowstone Park in mid-afternoon. Rose knew about it from geography lessons at school. It had lots of hot springs bubbling spouts of mud, and one, Old Faithful, which shot up seventy feet into the air every day, on the dot of half past five. You could set your watch by it. Some of the redwoods were a million years old and a mile high; there was one with a split in its trunk wide enough for a car to drive though. The campsite had lavatories adorned with funny signs, 'Jack—Jim' for the men, 'Joan—Jill' for the women, and strings of coloured lights slung between the trees.

They parked in the smallest site, away from the giant trucks and trailers, the Rest-U-Easy and Komfy Kampers, because Harold said they turned their generators on at night and it grew too noisy. When he began his daily shenanigans, sweeping out the van and rinsing the squashed flies off the windscreen, she tried to help by gathering up the newspapers from the driving seat. He told her to leave off; he could manage.

She was sitting on a hillock of grass nearby when a tall man with a red face approached.

'Hi, fellow travellers,' he shouted, 'Trust you're not too done in.' Harold said he wasn't.

'Praise be to God,' the man said. 'It's the wife's birthday and I aim to give her a good time. Be mighty pleased if you and your daughter would join us.'

'That's very kind . . .' began Harold, on the way to a refusal. The man took no notice. 'Sure could do with a helping hand,' he continued. 'There's stuff to be moved if you folks are up to it.' Reluctantly, Harold nodded; he wasn't brave enough to back out.

He spent less than an hour constructing tables from lengths of wood laid across boxes before returning to his cleaning. Rose stayed longer, gathering wild flowers and stuffing them into jam jars. The scarlet-faced man thanked her. His smile was warm, but his eyes were cold.

Nothing happened until dusk. Harold couldn't wait that long for food and fried himself two eggs on the paraffin stove. He looked careworn. Rose changed into a flowery skirt, and a blouse that had belonged to her mother. Harold drew attention to the moth hole in the collar.

The red-faced man was called Hayland. He was obviously on good terms with God, for he kept calling on Him to look after the meat roasting on the spit above the fire. His wife had big bosoms and went by the name of Saucy Sue. Owing to the attention Hayland gave to her buttocks, the patting, the fondling, Harold said it was out of the question that they were married. For once, Rose knew he was right. She had never, ever, seen Father touch Mother in a saucy way.

No more than two dozen people assembled under the fairy lights, in spite of the numerous tables. Hayland was disappointed, that was obvious. He kept wandering into the trees and shouting, 'Roll up, roll up. Everybody welcome.' And he drank a lot.

A man in a baseball hat attached himself to Harold. They sat outside the radiance of the fire, perched on upturned buckets, beer cans in hand, deep in conversation. A boy with the beginnings of a moustache questioned Rose about the Beatles. He was very hesitant and kept saying he was sorry if he was bothering her, but had she ever met them? She said she believed two of them had attended the art school round the corner from where she had once lived, but no, she had never actually seen them. His mother pushed in; she too was unable to utter a sentence without apologising for being intrusive. Within minutes, Rose was surrounded by stout women and muscular men expressing themselves so politely that she couldn't respond, not from the heart. The war came into it somewhere, the part her country had played. They made it sound as if she'd had a hand in it, even though she'd spent most of the Blitz asleep under the dining-room table. It was true that the British had conquered the Germans, but they wouldn't have done it if Mr Roosevelt hadn't lent money to Winston Churchill. Rose began to work out that the people around her weren't educated; they belonged to a different class from Mirabella, the Shaefers, or that man in the dressing gown who had thumped Harold.

She was dwelling on this when someone put an arm round her and steered her from the group. Fingers twiddled with her breasts. She pulled herself free and faced a man with a patch over one eye, the other eye winking suggestively. He said it would be sweet to get to know her better. Although it was an unusually nice way of expressing a need, she refused him with firmness. Too often, out of politeness, she had got herself into difficult situations. 'I'm so sorry,' she told him, 'thank you very much, but my husband would get cross.'

She was walking towards Harold when there was a loud disturbance. Hayland was swaying on a beer crate, bellowing for silence. 'That guy,' he yelled, pointing at someone in the darkness, 'my buddy, has had his house burnt to the ground.' Murmurs of commiseration rose from the guests.

Rose halted, eyes widening in joy; she was no longer alone.

They were sheltering in the porch of the church, to be out of the rain. She'd been telling him about the

*row there'd been on Sunday when Auntie Phyllis
had come for tea. Mother had cheated at rummy,
Father had hurled the playing cards across the brass
tray and Auntie Phyllis had gone home crying. 'Why,'
she asked Dr Wheeler, 'do people keep hurting each
other?' He said, 'If you want a compass to guide you
through life, you have to accustom yourself to looking
upon the world as a penal colony. If you abide by this
you'll stop regarding disagreeable incidents, sufferings,
worries and miseries as anything out of the ordinary.
Indeed, you'll realise that everything is as it should be;
each of us pays the penalty of existence in our own
peculiar way.'*

'I tell you,' bawled Hayland, spitting hatred, 'that
the next time I come across a fucking nigger I'll tear
his head from his shoulders. Are you with me?' A
boom of support echoed through the trees.

Harold and the man in the baseball cap were
now on either side of Rose, each gripping an elbow.
'Bastard . . . bastard,' Harold shouted, as they
hustled her away.

CHAPTER ELEVEN

The man who helped escort Rose from the birthday
gathering introduced himself as John Fury. He was
short and squat and dressed in an expensive, albeit
crumpled, white suit. By profession a lawyer, he
said he was now the head of a firm in Los Angeles.
He was also a shareholder in a horse farm in Santa
Ana, thirty miles outside the city. As a boy Harold
had owned a pony, which persuaded him that he
and Fury had something in common. They discussed

pedigrees, famous races, illustrious mounts.

Rose waltzed about, shadowy under the trees, skirt flapping. For once, she didn't butt in. Harold found it invigorating, conducting a conversation without being subjected to her banal interruptions.

It was a pity time was so short. Fury had an important case to prepare, something to do with fraud, and planned to drive off at first light. He was making for a homestead in the Salmon River mountains to question a woman who was thought to have relevant information.

Harold said, 'It's great to travel, isn't it? Shaking off familiar things livens the mind.'

'It sure does,' agreed Fury. 'Why, yesterday I had the most . . .' He stopped short and smiled sheepishly. Pushing back the brim of his cap, he rubbed his forehead.

'The most what?' prodded Harold.

'Odd experience . . . a sort of spiritual awareness. I guess it sounds crazy.'

'Not so,' Harold assured him.

'I stopped the car . . . it was in the afternoon . . . near a church. The building was nothing special, yet for some reason I felt impelled to go inside. I'm not a religious man . . . I mean, I believe in God, kind of, but I don't get worked up.'

'Me neither,' Harold said. He was aware that Rose had stopped dancing and was staring at them.

'There was some kind of service in progress,' continued Fury, 'and the organist was playing Bach's Mass in B Minor. You know the one I mean . . .' He began a melancholy humming.

'Not well,' Harold admitted.

'It was played at my father's funeral. I confess it reduced me to tears, but then I was very fond of my

103

old man . . . you know how it is.'

'No,' said Harold. 'I had too many—fathers, I mean.' Rose was grinning.

Fury bent forward on his stool. He said, 'I felt a pressure on my back, as if someone was touching me, urging me to stand, and when I did I felt such an overwhelming feeling of lightness that I thought I'd left my body behind.'

He stood up, arms outstretched on either side as if preparing for flight. Then, abruptly, he hunched over, chin on his chest. 'Seconds later,' he said, 'an incredible heaviness seized me, as if I was being pushed into the earth.'

Harold remained silent, unsure as to a proper response. He didn't look at Rose.

'Then I imagined I knew what it was . . . I was facing the Judgment seat . . . being weighed in the balance . . . and found wanting.'

'Jesus,' murmured Harold, but he wasn't thinking of God.

'The feeling's still with me,' Fury confided. 'Now I look at something quite ordinary, that stone, for instance—' he kicked the ground, dislodging soil, 'and realise it's just as important as myself. I told you it was crazy.' He was still massaging his brow, as if smoothing away thoughts. From the clearing beyond rose the sound of voices raggedly singing 'Happy Birthday' in honour of Saucy Sue.

Harold stayed mute. For the life of him he couldn't fathom how a man interested in horses could possibly talk such nonsense. Hearing the whine of a mosquito, he hurried to find his insect spray and spent some time in the camper making sure his skin was adequately protected.

When he returned, Rose was sitting cross-legged

104

at Fury's feet. He was spouting politics.

'. . . in 1964, McCarthy was elected Senator for Minnesota by the largest majority ever achieved by a Democrat. A man both bold and easily bored, he spoke of giving it all up and going back to being a college professor. Do you know he once referred to the Senate as a leper colony?'

Rose asked, 'Have you heard that song about a park in a rainstorm?'

Fury stared at her.

'MacArthur's Park is singing in the rain,' she warbled, 'I don't think that I can take it, for it took so long to bake it . . . oh no . . . la, la . . .'

Fury said, 'Though he has a cynical streak, he alone has always been nail-hard against the shoddy thinking in which our foreign policy is rooted, the muddy language in which it is justified—'

'It isn't explained what he was trying to cook,' Rose interrupted, 'particularly out in the open.'

'. . . the bloody consequences to which it has led,' persisted Fury. 'Vietnam, not least. He was a great friend of the poet, Robert Lowell . . . You've heard of him?'

'Who hasn't?' said Rose.

'He wrote verse himself. Do you know the lines: "Searching in attics and sheds of life, salvaging shards and scraps of truth, parts of dead poets, pieces of gods . . ."'

'Yes, yes,' she enthused. 'Who could forget a word of Mr Lowell's.'

'Lowell didn't write that,' corrected Fury. 'McCarthy did.'

Perched on his stool, Harold nudged Rose with his foot. She was smiling broadly, as she had been doing most of the evening. It was obvious she found Fury something of a joke, as amusing as that bigoted shit with the red face. To his relief she got to her feet and strolled into the trees. 'Not too far,' he warned, 'animals on the prowl.' Not that she deserved protection.

Fury wasn't in a hurry to leave. He confessed he found it uncomfortable sleeping in his car and had arrived too late to rent a cabin. He had a tent, but tents were prohibited on account of the grizzlies. He said he preferred to stay up all night, if Harold had no objection.

'None at all,' he said.

To his relief Fury kept off the subject of spiritual awareness and concentrated on McCarthy's merits and faults, that and the equally complex personality of Richard Nixon.

'He's come close, time and time again, to paranoia, but he never quite gives in to it. His style, don't you agree, is a perfect mixture of rage and caution?'

Harold said, 'Sure, but I still rate him.'

'He's been loathed ever since he tried to link Adlai Stevenson to Alger Hiss.' Suddenly, in the middle of expanding on this, Fury broke off. Looking into the darkness, he asked, 'I'm right, aren't I? She's older than she sounds.'

'Yes,' Harold joked, 'by about fifteen years.' He hoped Rose wasn't listening.

'What's the connection? You and she sure as hell don't have much in common.'

'I hardly know her,' he admitted, 'but we're both looking for the same person . . . a mutual acquaintance from the past.'

'Someone important?'

'To her, yes.'

'Unfinished business, perhaps,' said Fury. He was again rubbing his forehead.

'I have aspirins,' offered Harold. 'Would they help?'

Fury protested that he wasn't in pain, merely conscious of the discolouration of the skin above his left eye. He removed his hand and leaned closer. Harold adopted a sympathetic expression, although truth to tell he couldn't see anything out of the ordinary.

Fury said, 'I happened to be in Dallas the day JFK was killed. Business, you know. I had a client whose wife had set fire to their house in order to claim the insurance. She was one of those females who dislike men for their superiority. You know the sort?'

Harold grunted recognition.

'Leaving the court, I took a cab downtown only to find the street to the airport closed. I joined the crowds on foot, caught a brief glimpse of the motorcade, heard two shots and turned in time to hear a third. If I hadn't looked to my left, at a small boy who was bent down to quiet his dog, I'd have had a bullet through my head. As it was, it just grazed my temple. Luck, I guess.'

'I guess . . .' Harold said. He had an image of Oswald, eyes squeezed into slits, finger whitening as it tightened on the trigger.

'I wasn't called to give evidence. It was held that there was no need, the Oswald guy being caught so fast. Then Jack Ruby wrapped it all up and the whole business was considered closed. Not that it's done much good. If you need a sympathy vote you can't do better than climb on top of an assassinated brother, which is why Bobby will get the black

107

vote . . . on account of Luther King. Sudden death does a lot for politics.'

Harold said, 'Though not much for anything else.'

'I lost the case,' said Fury. 'The woman was too handsome, if you go for that sort. I don't. Too masculine . . . a touch of the Joan Crawfords.'

In his head, Harold saw Dollie's aquiline nose, the firm set of her jaw.

'Was she in that film,' he asked, 'in which a woman ran into the sea to end things . . . not from cowardice, just that she couldn't see the point any more?' The words out of his mouth, he was astonished at how like Rose he had sounded.

She came out of the darkness and without speaking climbed into the camper. She closed the door behind her.

'I'd be careful of that one,' Fury said. 'She could get you into trouble.'

He left at four thirty, just as light was beginning to leak into the sky. Before he drove off he gave Harold his address in both Los Angeles and Santa Ana.

'We see eye to eye,' he said. 'I'll be back in town around the second of June. Look me up.'

*   *   *

Harold brewed himself a cup of coffee and sat for an hour or more, conscious of the squawking of birds in the ceiling of trees. Then he went for a shower. On his return he found Rose up and dressed, though it was probable she'd slept in her clothes. To his surprise she'd cleared away the beer cans from the night before and was frying slices of bacon.

'Good to see you're hungry,' he said.

'Where are we going to next?' she asked. 'I'm worried there's not much time left.' She appeared subdued, quite unlike the giggling girl of yesterday.

He spread out the map and showed her the route he intended to follow: Salt Lake City, Salina, Panguitch, St George, Barstow and then LA. 'Barstow's in the desert,' he said.

'Desert?' she squealed. 'Aren't deserts dangerous? What if we run out of petrol?'

'It's not the Sahara. There's plenty of ghost towns and gas stations.'

'Ghosts?' she bleated.

'Just empty houses sinking into the sand.'

'How far away are we now from that place in Malibu?'

'Eight, nine hundred miles . . .'

'Oh heck,' she moaned, forking out the bacon and stuffing it between slices of bread, 'we'll never find him in time. He'll have moved on. He's always one step ahead.'

'Remember what Mirabella said,' he reminded her. 'If it's true that he's got something to do with the Democratic campaign, he'll be in Los Angeles for sure. And I reckon Fury will be of help. He's the sort of guy who's got connections.'

She said, munching on her sandwich, 'He was deeper than most, wasn't he? I liked him.'

'You sure didn't show it,' he snapped. He wanted to say more but a memory of his last visit to Salt Lake City took hold. He and Dollie had gone there to celebrate the birth of her sister's baby. That day, on a snow-capped Capitol Hill, John Kennedy had been sworn in as the youngest president ever.

They had stayed in a hotel, and a cat had got into their room and slept on their bed. Later that night he had climbed onto Dollie's body, but she had shrugged him away; on the second evening she had given in, lain submissive, then, violently, she'd drawn up her knee and jabbed him in the balls. She said the cat was to blame; it had stretched out a paw and scratched her ankle. Seeing the night was cold and they were under the covers, that didn't seem to touch the truth. The radio was on and above his cry of pain he'd heard Kennedy declaiming, *Ask not what your country can do for you, ask what you can do for your country.* He'd got up and hurled the cat into the corridor and she'd accused him of cruelty to animals.

'You should have a nap,' Rose said, tapping his arm with greasy fingers. 'You look very tired.'

He said, 'I'm not sure if that's a good idea.'

'Try not to dream,' she cautioned.

It was disconcerting the way she understood his fears.

*   *   *

Foolishly, he disregarded Rose's advice before taking to the road. Twice she had to thump his leg to keep him from nodding off. It wasn't just the lack of sleep that made him dozy; the unrelenting sunshine skittering off the silvery landscape dazzled his mind.

Then in late afternoon—they had got beyond Springfield in the state of Utah—there was the smallest of thuds followed by a shadow flash of something black beyond the windscreen. He braked abruptly. If he hadn't been slumped in his seat,

110

he'd have been flung against the dashboard. Sitting up, he registered a yellow tractor in a flat field drenched in sunlight, a house, white paint peeling, and a woman in green overalls standing beside a wooden fence. She was holding a brush dripping red paint.

The body slid across the slope of the hood and flopped out of sight. Rose was bent over her knees, making funny noises. He climbed out of the camper. The dog lay on its back, one paw raised, one eye fearfully alive. It was making the same sort of noise as Rose. Then it died.

Rose stumbled out onto the road. 'Is it dead?' she asked, clutching at his arm. He shrugged her away and, picking up the animal, walked towards the woman in the overalls. Rose followed him.

The woman's expression was sullen; she had hair on her lip. When he held out his burden she didn't look at it, just stuck out her hand and ground her thumb against her fingers, nails stained with globs of red paint. Harold struggled to take out his wallet. Not a word was said. The money handed over, the woman grabbed the dog by its back legs, stared at its dangling corpse, then slung it into the ditch beside the fence.

Walking back to the camper Rose said, 'She was an ignorant woman. You're not to take it to heart.'

He didn't reply. He climbed into the driving seat and sat there staring at the shimmering field.

She said, 'Some years ago, when my mum died, I had to go to the mortuary and look at her—'

'I thought it was a bundle of tumbleweed,' he interrupted.

'Just to say goodbye. Most people have to do that . . . not to identify them, just to send them on . . .'

'I wasn't given the chance,' he said. 'Chip Webster saw to that.'

'My mum was lying in a sort of Easter egg . . . paper frills all round her. I bent down to kiss her . . . her cheek was so cold that my tears bounced off onto the floor.'

Dismissively he waved his hand and leaned forward to start the engine.

'I'm not lying this time,' she said. 'It really did happen. And I noticed her nails were messy, so I went and bought some red nail varnish and coloured them.'

'To be ready for the next world,' he said. 'Thoughtful of you.'

'The good thing it did for me,' she persisted, 'was to make me believe that there's something beyond death. Her body was there but her soul wasn't.'

'Soul,' he spat, as though it were a swear word.

'Yes,' she said. 'Which had gone . . . and that's what made her dead.'

'For Christ's sake,' he muttered, and then drove at speed past the unfinished fence and the woman with the paint brush.

Darkness descended as the camper devoured the miles, nothing to be seen but black stretches of road stabbed by headlights. Then, out of nowhere, Harold recalled an afternoon in childhood when a man had taken him onto a beach somewhere near San Francisco, hand on his shoulder in a gesture of parental steering. The memory induced an odd lightness, a sensation of floating akin to the uplift of the expensive kite he'd tossed into the sky. Almost at once the paper aeroplane had swooped downwards and crumpled into the sand.

He braked, got out and bent over his knees. He

was drifting towards a splayed body spread across paving stones. He heard the word 'Wicked' resound in his mouth and vomited. Rose didn't interfere. He supposed she thought his upset was due to the mowing down of the dog.

CHAPTER TWELVE

Forty-eight hours later—they had fortified themselves with ham and eggs in a town called Bunkerville—they drove into the Mojave desert. Harold had taken onboard two canisters of water, one in case the engine of the camper started overheating, the other to avoid their perishing from thirst. Rose found their journey disappointing; she had been thinking of that film in which Lawrence of Arabia had faced sandy whirlwinds. There were too many bushes, too many clumps of vegetation; twice she saw a fox burrowing into the earth.

They passed through one of Harold's ghost towns, its sunblasted main street patrolled by a stetson-headed crowd in pursuit of the past. He said they were all tourists; possibly some of them had been born here. There was one house with an ancient wagon upturned on the dirt road outside, and another with a withered shirt still pegged to a washing line, strung from its collapsed veranda. Harold said it had been hung there for the benefit of sightseers. No one in that desperate yesteryear would have been careless enough to abandon an item of clothing.

Rose asked for a drink—it was very hot and she was sweating—but Harold told her to hang on, that he had a fan thing that swirled air around them. It got a shade cooler, but the expanse of flat landscape incrcased her need. She said, 'I could die.' Harold laughed; he didn't know that sand disturbed her mind. He was listening to an interview on the radio with a man who had been present a year ago when Robert Kennedy had delivered a speech to the Senate about Vietnam. *War*, Kennedy had roared, *was the vacant moment of amazed fear as a mother and child watched death by fire fall from an improbable machine sent by a country they barely comprehend.*

Rose said, 'What a complicated sentence.'

Harold told her to keep quiet.

Who are we to play the role of avenging angel? the voice on the radio asked.

After a perspiring two hours, Harold halted at an inn, refusing to drive further. He paid for separate rooms. They ate their supper in a crowded dining area, posher than usual and decorated with blown-up photographs of serious-looking men wearing old-fashioned clothes. Rose sat opposite a portrait of Mr Roosevelt. Their table was shoulder-close to an elderly couple; the man had a paper napkin tucked under his chin, a splodge of crimson ketchup staining the front. The woman hummed some sort of tune quite loudly—when she wasn't stuffing food into her mouth.

'Your hair's wet,' Harold said. He sounded censorious. Rose admitted she'd had a shower. 'I hate them, but I'd sweated like a pig.' He stared at her, his expression hard to interpret.

'What will you do,' she asked, trying to sound confident, 'once we've found Dr Wheeler? Will you stay in Los Angeles then drive all that way back on

114

your own?'

'I'm not sure . . .'

'I know he'll give you the money I owe you,' she reassured him.

'Of course,' he said. 'Wheeler could always be relied on to do the right thing.'

She was anxious to tell him yet again how grateful she was for his help, how she appreciated the liberal way he had forked out money. 'I'm not the easiest of people to get along with,' she admitted. 'It's to do with my background. I know you might have thought that we'd have had . . . you know . . . sex . . . most people do in these sort of circumstances, but—'

'Keep your voice down,' he urged. 'You want an end to it,' he murmured. 'So do I.'

She didn't know what end he was talking about, and didn't care. In her head she was walking towards a figure in a trilby hat.

Fingers dug into her elbow. 'I couldn't help noticing,' the humming woman said, 'that you have an English accent. Forgive the intrusion but my husband and I are making a trip to London next week. There's things we'd like to know, if you can spare the time.'

Harold refused to be drawn into the conversation. Twice the woman tried to include him, but he didn't respond. He and the man with the soiled napkin concentrated on the mess on their plates.

The woman told Rose that her name was Mrs Weiner; she was a theosophist, a believer in reincarnation. She was also a teller of fortunes, a reader of palms, of cards, indeed of any personal object belonging to someone requiring information

115

as to the past or the future. In the latter case, even a button would suffice. Feathers retrieved from pillows were the most reliable means of getting in touch with the dead, she said, but that was because they had to do with flight. Flight was migratory, spiritual.

Rose said, 'How interesting.' Her hand was in the pocket of her raincoat, thumb smoothing the photograph of Dr Wheeler.

'Theosophy is not such an isolated practice as you might think,' Mrs Weiner stressed. 'It began in America, but now it's a worldwide movement, strong in your own country. I'm due to attend a conference in London in two weeks' time in a place called St John's Wood. Is that out in the country? Will I need a sun hat, mosquito spray?'

'I doubt it,' Rose said.

'We're meeting in a house that was once occupied by Madame Blavatsky. You've heard of her?'

Rose shook her head.

'Everything's been paid for,' said the woman, 'plane fares, hotels. Is food still rationed? Will I need to take sweeteners?'

It was strange, Rose thought, how someone so knowing about time, both gone and yet to come, should be so short on knowledge to do with the here and now. She said, 'The hotels will look after you, but it would be wise to take a few jumpers and an umbrella.'

As she spoke, Harold got up and announced he was off to his room. He stretched out a hand as if about to stroke her hair, then abruptly walked away. She watched him thread his way past the tables and walk out into the night.

Mrs Weiner leaned closer. In half an hour's time there was to be a gathering of like-minded people in a room adjacent to the motel's checking-in desk. They were part of a group on their way to a theosophist conference in Arroyo Grande. This evening's discussion would fix on attempts to unearth events that lay buried, forgotten. 'The persons we once were,' Mrs Weiner intoned, 'whom we no longer remember, hold the most secrets.' Admittance was free. She felt sure Rose would find it stimulating.

Rose decided to go, mostly because she had nothing better to do. There were no more than nine people assembled in the side room, all female save for the husband who had spilt ketchup down his front, and a fat man wearing a bow tie, who was sitting beside Mrs Weiner.

Rose took a seat at the back and then moved forward; she didn't want to draw attention to herself by looking solitary. The proceedings began with a prayer to Him on High followed by a rendering of 'I Want To Hold Your Hand' sung without accompaniment by an elderly lady in a coal-black wig. Rose wanted to laugh. Then the man in the bow tie pointed at a thin figure wearing a blue dress. 'You've no need to stand,' he said, 'I know what's troubling you. You have an illness.'

'Yes, yes,' squeaked blue dress, struggling upright. 'Help me.'

'It's the evil cancer,' bow tie declared, voice flat, empty of sympathy. 'You gotta accept it as a disorganisation of cells, not as a punishment from God. There is nothing you can do now, except rejoice that you have time to sort out the conflicts that remain in your life. Hallelujah.'

117

'Thank you, thank you,' cried blue dress, apparently pleased to hear that the end was just round the corner.

Rose was convinced the woman wasn't genuine, that she'd been planted there to show how far-seeing were the minds of those in charge. She didn't think the second and third victims were real either, although their lost memories were more airy-fairy, more conducive to sparking the imagination. Number two was asked by Mrs Weiner if she had something in her past to do with a man on crutches.

'He's not tall, wears a red scarf round his neck . . . no, green not red, and he's trying to tell you something.'

Number two said, 'I don't remember anyone on crutches.'

'Think, think,' Mrs Weiner prodded. 'I see a tall building and a swirl of cloud. No . . . no, it's smoke . . . and I see a figure standing at an open window.'

'Oh . . . oh . . .' cried number two, arms raised in sudden shock. She'd recalled a fire, and her grandfather throwing himself out of a window, fortunately only two floors up from a spacious ledge. Grandfather had lived on, albeit with a limp, so it wasn't a proper tragedy. The important bit, what he'd wanted to tell her, wasn't divulged.

Number three was foreign and difficult to understand. She wore dangling earrings. The man in the bow tie brought up the subject of an old car breaking down, and of a child watching it being pushed down a road. The foreign woman shook her head, the lobes of her ears swishing metal. There was a crossroads, bow tie prompted, and a man had come forward to help. He had then dragged a

118

female, screaming, into the bushes and committed an offence. The child had seen legs without stockings thrashing about in the leaves.

A break was called after this to give the child, now middle-aged, time to recover after she blurted out that it was her mother she'd seen being taken into the undergrowth. Paper handkerchiefs were supplied.

Rose knew that she was going to be targeted next. She stayed because she found it amusing, this daft pretence at unearthing memories. What would she do, she wondered, if Mrs Weiner spirited up an image of sand spilling onto the head of Billy Rotten? She needn't have worried. All that was directed at her was a description of a young man in a yellow sweater galloping past on a black horse.

'Bright yellow?' she queried, adopting a thoughtful expression. She looked round the dull room, walls painted white, not a picture on display, its low ceiling studded with spotlights. 'He's with you at an important time,' said Mrs Weiner.

Rose said, 'I'm not into horses.' It wasn't true. As a child she had often sat on the back of the brown mare that had pulled the milkman's cart round the village streets, but that animal had never moved faster than a sedate trot. 'You don't know him,' Mrs Weiner acknowledged, presumably referring to yellow sweater, 'but you have a lot in common.'

Rose skedaddled out of the door, a hand covering her eyes as though hiding tears; she was avoiding the collection plate.

It was almost dark outside and still warm. A stretch of ground sloped down to a semi-circle of trees hung with lanterns, moths flickering like snowflakes above the tangerine lights. Drawn to the sight, she approached and stopped; she had noticed a shadowy couple locked in an embrace. The image was romantic. She hoped their hearts beat in tune. She herself, in all her years of sexual encounters, had known true love but once. 'A dirty union between underage fornicators,' Mother had labelled it, which was why it was necessary for the resulting infant to be given away. Mothers could always be depended upon to know what was best.

*   *   *

Rose was in her room, partially undressed, when there was a knock at the door. She asked who it was and heard Harold's voice. When she let him in, he was fiddling with the undone flies of his shorts, stuffing his erect penis into a condom. He reached her and pushed her down onto the bed. She could have jumped up or punched him away, but did neither. He lay on top of her, his tongue swashing about in her ear. Above the roar of the sea, she heard him mutter, 'Help me . . . I must . . . I can . . .'

The ease with which he entered her probably made him think she was aroused. He wasn't to know that she was one of those females whose bodies were ready for penetration even when their minds were closed. It was over in seconds. He left almost immediately.

She slept without dreaming, and was surprised on going outside the next morning to find the motel surrounded by armed police. There were more of them patrolling the area under the trees. Fantasising, she imagined that Harold's behaviour had provoked an arrest. But then, as she reached the breakfast room, he ran towards her and took her arm. 'There's been a murder,' he said, 'down by the stream.' He looked shaken. A woman's body had been found at dawn, throat slashed. She was the wife of a blues singer performing in Las Vegas. Her father, poor man, was the motel's manager.

They were about to sit down for breakfast when the spiritualist woman, Mrs Weiner, approached and seized Rose's arm.

'You see,' she hissed, cheeks aflame with excitement, 'we really do see things.'

'Things?' echoed Rose.

'Death,' Mrs Weiner said. 'That woman last night who was dragged into the bushes by some blackie . . .'

Harold interrupted, tone censorious. 'We don't know he was coloured. You have no right to assume that he was . . . I guess the name Abe Lincoln means nothing to you.'

Mrs Wiener wasn't at all cowed. 'It does,' she snorted. 'It was he who said that niggers should never marry whites or ever be given social or political equality.'

Harold stepped backwards as though struck.

'The mother of the woman with earrings didn't die,' Rose said, pushing Mrs Weiner away, 'she just got interfered with. You're confused.'

She steered Harold to a table near the door. His face had no colour. She said, 'It takes time for people to view things differently. Things that are now considered bad will one day be thought of as normal.' She wasn't at all sure what she meant.

She consumed a big breakfast, even the hash-browns, and chatted to Harold in a relaxed manner. Admiring his green striped shirt, one she hadn't seen before, she said, 'It would be better if

121

you fastened the top three buttons. Your mosquito bites look as though you've gone down with the plague.'

He looked at her, eyes hurt. Rose patted his hand. It was easy to talk to him so frankly now that she no longer owed him anything. Telling him she wanted to see what the weather was like, she stood up brusquely and left to go outside. Dazzled by sunlight she heard a shriek of pain above the slamming of the door behind her.

CHAPTER THIRTEEN

The damage to Harold's hand was not life-threatening, although the pain after that initial clamping was ferocious. Holding his hand up in the air was helpful, something learnt from an injury received as a child while playing basketball. It was his mother, eyes glazed, a glass of whisky in one hand, who had shoved his fingers towards the clouds.

The blood issuing from his squashed nails upset Rose; there were even tears in her eyes. He was about to reassure her that it wasn't that bad when he realised it might be advantageous to let her think it was serious. She had been implying over breakfast that they should bypass Los Angeles and drive straight to Malibu. He hadn't told her that a previous telephone call made it clear that Wheeler had booked out three days ago.

Rose insisted someone should look at his hand. The manager of the inn sent for a member of staff who bathed the crushed fingers in disinfectant before applying a bandage. A sling was produced but Rose objected to its use. She said he wouldn't be able to hold the wheel, not properly.

'I'm not thinking of driving,' he told her, 'not for a day or two. It wouldn't be safe.'

'That's all right,' she said. 'I'll hitch-hike.'

'You can't,' he protested. 'It's dangerous.'

'You don't have to worry,' she retorted, 'I went all over England in lorries when I was a child.'

'To hell with England,' he shouted, 'this is America. Set foot alone on the road and you could end up stabbed, shot, strangled . . .' He was about to add 'raped' when he remembered his own behaviour of the night before. Wincing, he clutched the wrist of his damaged hand. For once she didn't argue, nor did she walk away. He reckoned she was feeling guilty at the harm she'd done.

They remained at the inn for two nights. Rose said that it would be cheaper to sleep in the van, but he argued that with the temperature now above 100 degrees it would be impossible to sleep without air conditioning; he didn't mention that she stank of perspiration.

He insisted she come with him to see the historic railway station, Casa del Deserto, now derelict, that stood beside the line that had linked Kansas City with the Pacific. She gave him a funny look, but followed him as he strode down Main Street. Once there, she stared at the ruined facade while he explained that a century ago the region had been famous for mining gold and silver.

'Why does everything have a foreign name?' she asked.

'Because most of the land belonged to Mexico before gold was discovered.'

123

'The gold rush,' she chirped. 'I saw Charlie Chaplin in the film.'

'When the mines went dry the immigrants moved on. That's why there's so many ghost towns.'

She began to burble away about the greed of people and how everyone got ruined by wealth. 'My father,' she said, 'was made bankrupt in 1929. He was so into money that he didn't think about moonlight or flowers.'

Harold turned his head away and gazed up at the sea-blue sky. He wondered how much longer he would be able to put up with her childish and ignorant pronouncements.

'We had a rose garden,' she said, 'that he let die from lack of fertiliser. My mother cried.'

'Wheeler has money,' he interrupted, and added, 'Me too.'

It shut her up. After all, where would she be without his own healthy investments?

On the third morning, Rose didn't answer his knock at her door. Alarmed, he hurried into the breakfast room, then out into the street. She was sitting on the veranda of a clapboard shack, talking to herself. He rebuked her for wandering off and she told him she'd met a nice man who'd taught her a song. He pulled her upright and marched her back into the inn. She only had coffee this time and didn't ask the usual questions about how long it was going to take to get to Malibu. She lit a cigarette, smoked half of it and stuffed the remainder into her raincoat pocket.

'That black man said there's been a shooting on a farm about a mile away,' she said. 'A woman in a wheelchair. She's not dead.'

He remarked that shootings were commonplace;

looking down at his plate he heard the increased thudding of his heart.

'And he taught me a song,' Rose said, and recited:

> *We grub de bread,*
> *Dey gub us de crust*
> *We skim de pot,*
> *De gub us de liquor*
> *And say dat's good enough for niggers.*

'For God's sake,' he hissed, 'there are riots all over the States at the moment, mostly on account of prejudiced people like you. You can't use that word.'

'I'm sorry,' she faltered, looking genuinely upset, 'I just thought it was an interesting song written by slaves. They used the word niggers . . .'

'Even the names of hills and rivers that once contained the word have been changed,' he told her. 'That's how unusable it is.'

'But we passed through a place called Nigger Creek . . .'

'Leave it,' he said, but she wouldn't.

'It's no different from you being called a Yankee,' she shouted, 'you're all American.' Then she rambled on about an English politician who had apparently got into trouble for saying there were too many coloured people coming into Great Britain. 'It was only a couple of weeks ago,' she said. 'He warned that if it carried on we'd see the Thames foaming with blood.'

Curtly he told her to collect her belongings, and strode out to the camper.

*　　　*　　　*

Los Angeles was ninety-three miles away. Harold avoided Route 66 and chose deserted country roads. There was nothing to be seen from the window but farmland edged by the swooning blur of sun-drenched mountains. After an hour, he came to a halt. Now that he was near the end of his journey, his elation was mixed with fear. It would have helped to confide in his travelling companion, but that's all she was.

Rose asked what was wrong. He thought of saying they were out of gas. Looking at her face— her pale lips appeared to be quivering—for one crazy moment he felt it might be possible to tell her the truth. But that was out of the question. She would hardly allow him to harm her precious Dr Wheeler.

He said, reaching under the seat, 'I need a drink. My hand hurts.'

She said, 'Go ahead. It'll do you good.' She even unscrewed the top for him and would have held it to his mouth if he hadn't snatched the bottle away. He was aware she was watching him, her mouth curved in a patient smile. 'Does drink help?' she asked.

'Nothing helps,' he snapped. 'How could it?'

Reluctantly, he offered her the bottle but she said she didn't really need it, that she had funny enough thoughts as it was. She lived, she confessed, mostly in the past. The here and now meant little to her; it was what made her so unusual. That struck him as comic, she being so unaware of the impression she gave, but he didn't laugh.

'I wouldn't have taken you for a drinker,' she

126

said. 'You're not the type. You don't have things that torment you.'

Gazing out of the open window, he saw an image of Wheeler in an invalid chair float across the blinding sky.

Rose was talking to herself again. Seeing his look, she told him she was arguing with her father. She said she often did this because, being dead, he couldn't answer back. He didn't comment; he was trying to work out where and how he might confront Wheeler. If Wheeler was involved in the Democratic presidential campaign he'd hardly be found wandering around on his own. Ideally, their meeting needed to be in a solitary place, somewhere so isolated that they wouldn't be seen, otherwise there was the danger that someone might come up with a description . . . even a snapshot. Perhaps he should shave off his beard.

'Funny thing is,' Rose said, 'although he was a bully, he was a terrible crybaby. Once, he went all over Southport pressing sixpences into the hands of those he called our gallant boys in blue . . .'

It might, he thought, be a good idea to telephone John Fury.

'They were soldiers from the new hospital down by the promenade. My father told them that he was proud of them, that they were the walking wounded . . .'

Fury, Harold reasoned, would know where Kennedy and his gang were likely to be.

'Afterwards it turned out there was nothing wrong with them, nothing wounded that is. They were soldiers all right, Mother said, but they'd all caught a nasty men's disease from being in the army.'

127

He pictured Wheeler's face, his expression, the image searing into his mind.

Rose said, 'I'm scared about seeing him. It's been so long. What if he's not the same person?'

It jolted him, her having the same thoughts as himself.

Thirty minutes later he parked in a campsite off the San Bernardino Freeway. Clutching his hand he said he needed to rest, but first he must make a telephone call. Rose objected, on the grounds that he should stop thinking about stocks and shares and concentrate on his health. 'My health,' he retorted, 'is dependent on money.'

A woman answered his call and informed him that Fury would be back the following day, the second of June. He could be reached at his Santa Ana address. On his return, he was astonished to find that Rose had unfurled the mattress and hung up the mosquito net. As she was being so helpful he decided to tell her what he planned to do the next day. He assured her that Los Angeles was pretty close to Santa Ana and that the sooner they made contact with Fury and got to know the exact location of Senator Kennedy the sooner they'd track down Wheeler. Rose made no comment, just pulled a face.

CHAPTER FOURTEEN

Santa Ana had pretty houses adorned with white awnings, along streets parading under palm trees. It reminded Rose of Southport, though there weren't any fairy lights. Coming round a corner, the camper had to swerve out of the path of a small boy walking his dog. Harold swore.

Fury's farm was a mile or so out of town, down a dirt track gloomy with foliage. Ahead lay a courtyard edged with what Rose took to be stables, on account of a horse's head poking out. There was also a parched two-storied house, paint peeling, bordering a stretch of butter-coloured grassland. She didn't really register the scene because she was concentrating on Dr Wheeler. For too many days he had drifted away, ceased to talk, become nothing but a shadow. She hoped this was because they were about to meet, but feared it had to do with him being dead. It wasn't easy to make contact with the departed, not unless one had watched them go.

They were approached by a young man in a yellow sweater who was lugging sacks. Rose didn't like the way Washington Harold treated him. To get over his curt command to be taken to see Fury, she smiled a lot and even winked. Just because he was foreign didn't mean he didn't have feelings.

Fury was out, but he had a wife, a small woman wearing jodhpurs and spectacles. She was called Philopsona, or something like that. She lived most of the year on the horse farm in order to take care of her elderly mother who, she confided, could no longer live in Los Angeles after being traumatised by events some twenty years before. Her mother sat in a chair overlooking the fields, dressed in a nightie and a straw hat, clutching a woolly rabbit and the remains of a charred handbag.

When Fury at last appeared he played glad to see them. He shook hands with Harold and kissed Rose on the cheek. His lips were cold. Soon after, he and Harold walked out into the yard, leaving

129

Rose alone with the mother-in-law. Philopsona was busy raking up horse pooh from the path below the house.

There was an enlarged photograph on the sitting-room wall of a building on fire, and another of a city in ruins. Rose was turning away from them when Mrs Fury's mother said, 'I was there.' Her voice was confident, her eyes glittering; she was someone still endeavouring to make sense of the present. Rose wasn't surprised; most of her own life had been spent dwelling on the wounds of the past.

'My mother is dead,' the woman said, which, considering her age, was only to be expected. 'She was buried in a pink nightgown and my Pa put pink roses on her grave owing to having humped her into the ground.'

'It must have looked nice,' said Rose.

The woman urged her to come closer. 'Pink has to do with lusts of the flesh . . . and my Pa told me that the name Rose is in memory of the woman of Babylon.'

Rose tried to look interested. 'Babylon . . .' she murmured.

'She was the first prostitute.'

A tap dance of hooves sounded from the cobbles beneath the window, followed by a shrill whistle. Leaning out, Rose saw the young man in the sweater beckoning her to come down. 'I'll be back,' she reassured the old woman.

Fury wanted Rose to see his horses. He had, he said, been breeding them for twenty years, owing to an interest fostered in childhood by a distant relative. It was the smell of them he liked, the heady mixture of sex and speed. There was another man with him, a Mr Silver, who had a pot

130

belly and wore a bow tie. He acted very friendly to Rose; whenever he spoke to her his arm circled her shoulder.

Rose reached out to touch the solitary animal. It immediately reared backwards, nostrils quivering. It was, said Fury, awaiting an injection to protect it from some horsey disease.

'It sure recognises a wild spirit,' joked Mr Silver, pulling Rose close.

Before they returned to the house, Fury took Harold to one side and babbled into his ear for some minutes.

'He's apologising for his wife,' Silver told Rose. 'She's on the rough side.'

'Rough?' echoed Rose.

'He was only eighteen when he met her. It was a love match, at first, but she's hardly the typical lawyer's wife. That's why it's convenient to have her living in Santa Ana.'

'What's wrong with her?' asked Rose, intrigued.

'Mostly her language,' provided Silver. 'That and her generosity. She keeps giving money away.'

Philopsona cooked them lunch, the ingredients home-grown, even the chicken. The birds, she trumpeted, were her pride and joy, each one with a name and fondled from birth. She never allowed anyone but herself to wring their necks. 'It wouldn't be right,' she assured Rose. 'They need somebody they can fucking trust!' The one they were about to devour was called Nessie.

While waiting for the meal to be served, Rose again examined the photographs on the wall. Below, on the mantelpiece, she admired a green ornament.

'It's a frog,' Philopsona told her. 'My Pa liked

131

frogs.'

'It's a toad,' corrected Rose. 'Frogs don't have toes.'

'What?' said Philopsona. 'Who gives a shit?'

The food served, her mother, seated at the end of the table, kept picking up pieces and smashing them down with her fork.

'I only like fat,' she told Rose, 'I need the dribble.' At which, her daughter shouted, 'For Christ's sake, Ma, keep your goddamn mouth shut.' Seeing Rose's shocked expression, Philopsona patted her knee and confided that Ma was used to such treatment.

'At least,' she said, 'she knows she's being noticed.'

It turned out that Mr Silver was attached to the Senate, in an advisory post. He knew more about the current whereabouts of the Democrats than Fury. He informed them he had held a prominent position in J.F. Kennedy's election campaign, and been involved in the investigation into his death.

'Killing,' interrupted Harold.

'I knew the Kennedy family pretty well,' Silver boasted. 'I stayed with them on a couple of occasions, once in Boston and another time at their place in Palm Beach. I'm not likely to forget that particular weekend . . . it could have been my last. None of us knew about it at the time, but a guy was parked outside in a car packed full of dynamite. Early on Sunday morning—we were about go off to church—Jack went out onto the balcony, followed by Jackie and the kids. But the fellow drove off. After he was caught, he said he'd changed his mind because he wasn't into harming children. He ended up in a mental hospital. When told what he'd intended to do, Rose Kennedy didn't bat an eyelid.'

'Rose,' echoed Rose, thrilled.

'She's a cold woman, a woman who's never showed affection to any of her children . . . it's what made Jack such a chaser of girls. He needed their attention, and sex was the quickest way he knew how to get it.'

'She didn't have it easy,' Fury argued, 'she had eight other kids . . . one of them retarded . . . and that bastard of a husband.'

Silver agreed there'd been little sunshine in her life, Joe senior being such a hard guy, obsessed by money and power. Though bitterly opposed to the war, he'd expressed pride when his boy had volunteered to fly on bombing raids. 'I guess,' he said, 'that he thought it showed the Kennedys weren't yellow. But it near finished him off when Joe junior got blown up. Guilt mostly. He never forgave himself, or Roosevelt for that matter, who he accused of being manipulated by a rotten bunch of Jews and Communists. I was present the day he attacked Truman, for backing what he called "that crippled son of a bitch who killed my son". I remember the occasion because the sunlight was streaming through the windows and Joe's head was circled with a halo. He snarled that if he were Roosevelt he'd commit suicide.'

'Hubert Humphrey made the same mistake last year,' said Fury. 'Remember the photograph he had taken linking arms with that freak Lester Maddox . . .'

'Humphrey loves people like an alcoholic loves booze,' remarked Harold. Though she didn't know who he was talking about, Rose thought that was quite witty.

'Neither old Joe nor Rose shed a tear after being told that Jack had been shot,' said Silver. 'Nor did they ask for details. But by that time old Joe's brain had gone.'

'I wouldn't have asked either,' said Rose. 'Best left in the dark.'

'At least,' Fury said, 'it was easy to nail the guy who killed Jack.'

'It sure was lucky,' Mr Silver acknowledged, 'that Oswald was spotted going into a movie theatre.'

'Even luckier,' barked Harold, 'to have Jack Ruby standing by with a gun.'

There was a sudden silence. Rose was aware that the occupants of the table, particularly Fury, had become uncomfortable. Then Philopsona, worried that her chicken wasn't being appreciated, launched into an account of how easy it was to extinguish life.

'They approach,' she said, 'cluck, and when seized dip down and stay mute . . . they goddamn well freeze. They know what's going to happen.'

'Unlike JFK,' said Harold, at which Silver banged the table and proposed a toast, 'To Robert Kennedy,' he bellowed, 'soon to be the great leader of a great country.'

Harold didn't raise his glass.

The lunch over, Fury invited his guests to come for a ride. 'If he suggests you break into a gallop,' Silver warned Rose, 'just keep a tight grip on the reins. If the horse doesn't respond, slide off.'

He himself wasn't joining them, having five years before sustained a fracture of the skull after being tossed going over a gate. It had happened, he said, because he'd been brought up on a farm and been deluded into feelings of authority where animals were concerned. But it wasn't the injury that deterred him, more that he was still smarting from the medical bills he'd had to pay.

'Rose can't go,' Harold said, holding up his hand as though directing the traffic.

'But I want to,' she protested, 'it'll be fun.'

'You're not insured,' he snapped.

'Then why,' she retorted, 'have you let me travel thousands of miles in that van?'

'She can take Gingernuts,' said Fury. 'She's so old she can hardly walk, let alone trot.' Outside, the fields sparkled like glass beneath a violently blue sky. It was hard to breathe. A black woman with huge bare arms harnessed three munching horses. She had a cross dangling from a string about her neck and no shoes on her feet. Rose thanked the woman profusely for helping her into the saddle. She noticed that Fury stroked the woman's thighs before mounting.

It soon became apparent that Rose's horse was indeed without energy. It stopped frequently to pluck at the grass. After half an hour, by which time Harold and Fury were out of sight, it lay down, leaving Rose with her feet scraping the ground. She kicked at it, gently, but it ignored her.

Dismounting, she wandered back over the fields, amusing herself by seeing how far she could spit. Dr Wheeler had been tops at spitting. Once, in the churchyard, he'd spat clear over three graves. She'd tried too, but her phlegm had landed in a pot of daffodils, at which he'd tossed the contaminated soil into the pine trees. Tributes to the dead, he'd said, should be treated with respect. At the time, she'd considered coming back to the cemetery on her own and moving the pot to the tunnel on the shore, to the sandy darkness where an old man had once crouched. Governments and generals, she reasoned, were always attending memorial services to those they had pushed into death. Later she'd changed her mind—it would have amounted to theft.

Entering the stable yard she saw yellow sweater hunched on the veranda steps, smoking a cigarette. At her approach he jumped to his feet and ran towards her. 'The horse,' he shouted, 'where is your horse?' She was surprised at how well he spoke, barely a trace of a funny accent.

'It sat down,' she told him. 'It'll come back, won't it? They're like dogs.'

He didn't reply, just stared at the meadow beyond, expression worried. His face was brown, though not from the sun, his hair black and curly. It was cheeky of her, but she asked if he could spare her a cigarette. 'I'll give you one back,' she reassured him. Reluctantly, he left off scanning the horizon and indicated the pack on the steps. 'Thank you, thank you,' she cried, oozing gratitude, but he had already opened the gate and was striding off into the field.

The packet was almost full. Guiltily she removed two and, stuffing them into her pocket, scurried round the side of the house. Mr Silver, dissolving in a pool of sunlight, was weeing through a barred gate. Philopsona sat hunched on the grass, hands covering her face. For a moment Rose thought this was to avoid the sight of private parts, but then the woman moaned loudly and beat at her eyes with clenched fists.

She was backing away when Silver called out, 'Wait . . . nearly done.' Doing up his trousers. he said, 'Don't go, there's things I want to know.'

She asked, 'What's wrong with her?'

'Nothing,' he replied, a bead of sweat bouncing from his eyebrow. Taking her arm he steered her in the direction of the house. 'How well do you know John Fury?' he asked. 'When did you get together?'

'We're not together,' she corrected. 'I hardly know him . . . we met in a forest. I'm with Harold, but we're not together either . . . not really. He's just helping me find someone.'

'For what reason?'

'Is Mrs Fury sick?'

'This person you're both looking for,' demanded Silver, 'does she live round here?'

'Please,' she said, 'I'm looking for a man . . . he's nothing to do with Harold, just me.'

Reaching the house, she pulled away from him and sat on the steps to light a cigarette. He stood over her, legs splayed wide, eyes searching her face. His trousers hadn't been fastened properly, the top button left undone.

'Why would Harold want to help you if you're not together?' he persisted.

He wasn't going to give up, she could tell. It was Dr Wheeler's opinion that those in need of answers were trying to deal with the darkness to come, Napoleon being an example, though she couldn't remember why.

She said, 'When I was a child I met a man who helped me into adulthood.'

'What does that mean?'

'He lifted the things that weighed me down.'

'What things?' said Silver drily, lowering himself onto the step beside her.

From the yard below came a stutter of hooves as the riders returned. The black woman came out of the stables and helped Harold dismount. He was looking directly at Rose, his face angry. 'Where the hell did you go?' he shouted.

She ignored him and ran towards Fury. 'Your wife isn't well,' she blurted. 'She's crying.' Fury looked at Silver, who nodded and pointed towards the side of the house. Harold seized Rose and shook her. He asked her again where she had gone. 'Don't you realise what it looked like,' he thundered. 'You could have been lying unconscious somewhere.'

'But I wasn't,' she retorted, eyeing his sunburnt nose, 'it wasn't my fault the horse got weary.' He would have jostled her again if Silver hadn't intervened; taking Harold by the elbow he propelled him up the steps.

She loitered in the yard, remembering what Dr Wheeler had taught her about confrontation, particularly if one was in the wrong. 'Become forgetful,' he'd advised, 'especially if it's serious.' She stood there, the sun beating down on her head, imagining how it would be once they were reunited. Would he look the same? She stroked the photograph in her pocket, the one taken at Charing Cross station the day he'd left her. They'd shake hands, not kiss. She'd wear her polka-dot dress, even though she didn't think he'd ever seen her in anything other than slacks and a raincoat . . . she'd stuck to these because he said they suited her. Her slacks were new, but the raincoat was the same. Once, years ago, she'd tried to press her lips to his cheek and he'd pushed her away firmly, but not roughly. He hadn't said anything, but she'd realised she shouldn't try that again, not ever. She'd wear her raincoat with the dress . . . just in case his

138

expression showed disapproval.

Fury came into the yard, his arm round Philopsona; she wasn't sobbing any more. Neither of them looked at Rose as they crossed towards the steps. She stayed where she was, her back to the house, fingers still touching the photograph, until Mr Silver shouted from the window that Harold was in a better mood and that she should come up.

There were three bottles of wine on the table, two of them empty, and a packet of cigarettes nudging a silver lighter. There were no glasses, only tea cups. Harold was slumped in his chair, eyes shut. Philopsona wasn't there, nor the old mother, just the woolly rabbit, glass eyes ablaze under the window sunlight. Fury and Silver were talking about some man who had been murdered. Lots of people had been upset. Silver maintained that the dead man was a secondary rather than a primary target of a plot aimed to cause unrest. Colour, he asserted, didn't really come into it.

'We learned about that at school,' interrupted Rose. 'The first attempt didn't work and the chap who fired the gun gave up and sat down on the pavement.'

They stared at her. She thought they must be impressed by her knowledge of history.

'Then, owing to some pile-up in the traffic, the car came back and the next shot worked—on the wife as well. They were archdukes. The Pope fainted when he heard the news. It turned out that the killer was backed by a secret society known as the Black Hand.'

Silver giggled. Fetching a cup, he poured her some wine. Fury rose and said he ought to see if his wife was all right. When he'd gone, Silver asked

Rose if she was curious to know what was wrong with Philopsona. She said that she wasn't, that it was none of her business. He took no notice and launched into an explanation, not much of which she could follow. It had to do, he confided, with a substance, a kind of medicine which was pretty much in demand in the 1950s—underground, that is. MK-Ultra, the code name for a secret CIA interrogation project he'd been involved in, had planned to use it on the communists of North Korea who, backed by Russia, were advancing on Seoul. 'It would have been dropped from the air,' he said, 'a method of attack far less expensive than sending in troops. The Chinese and North Koreans were already using their own mind-control techniques on US prisoners of war and something was urgently needed by way of retaliation . . .' The substance had been tested on jailbirds and prostitutes, not that they knew it—here Silver smiled, the smile of a man recalling happier times. It didn't harm them, he reassured her, merely rendered them incapable of doing much more than singing and reciting poetry.

'Poetry,' echoed Rose.

'Personally,' Silver said, 'I'm glad they abandoned the idea and resorted to killing the bastards.'

'I took part in a rally two months ago,' she recounted, 'in Trafalgar Square, in support of North Vietnam. Three hundred people were arrested. I don't remember any poems.'

'Fury,' Silver said, 'being that sort of guy, had some of the stuff in his desk and unfortunately Philopsona, having heard how it reduced stress and violence in those exposed to childhood suffering . . .'

'Childhood suffering . . .' echoed Rose.

'. . . tried it. It had the opposite effect and for a time she was subject to fits, which only gradually subsided. For the past three years they've not been so regular.'

Rose wanted to ask if it was the medicine that caused Philopsona to swear and give away money, but at that moment Harold opened dazed eyes and murmured that he was sorry . . . very sorry.

'We ought to leave,' she urged, tapping the table. 'We've got to get to Malibu.'

He nodded and dozed off again.

Silver said he understood that the guy she and Harold were searching for would probably be staying at the Ambassador Hotel. 'I guess it won't be easy to gain entry,' he told her, 'not with the Kennedy entourage waiting to hear the results of the primary.'

He was very kind. He promised he'd arrange to get them a couple of passes, either before they left or via Fury, who by that time should be back in his office.

When Fury returned from seeing to his wife he said he would be in Los Angeles on the fifth, Philopsona being on the road to recovery.

'Goody, goody,' cried Rose.

Then a heated discussion began between the two men to do with Israel and the Arabs. Fury said that the Jews were out to extend their borders by force, that they wanted to unseat a man called Nasser because he was a lightning rod for Arab unity, and that they wanted the Cold War to continue. It was Israel who had killed President Kennedy, because nothing could be achieved as long as he remained in the White House.

141

'Oswald wasn't a Jew,' shouted Silver.

Rose said, 'My dad hated Jews . . . and Catholics . . . and the Salvation Army.'

'The Senate is riddled with Jews, as you well know,' Fury persisted.

'That's bullshit,' bellowed Silver, shaking a finger at Fury. 'The assassination was the demented act of a disturbed individual, the victim of a shitty upbringing.' Rose was impressed by his acknowledgment of parental fault and nodded vigorously, but neither of them noticed. As far as they were concerned, she wasn't there.

She went and sat in the old mother's chair by the window, tugging at the ears of the rabbit and watching yellow sweater going in and out of the stables. She tried to put Dr Wheeler in the yard but he stayed hidden in her head. Presently, Fury and Silver having abandoned the table in search of more wine, she got up, slid a cigarette out of the packet, pocketed the lighter and hurried out the door. Yellow sweater was standing in the open, looking up at the sky, arms outstretched.

He wasn't easy to talk to, nor was he all that grateful when she handed him the fag. She reckoned his unease was due to him being a foreigner, and asked if he liked looking after horses so far away from home.

'This is my home,' he replied. 'I came here twelve years ago, and I do more than look after horses. I am a jockey.'

'Of course you are,' she affirmed. She would have said more but he stared at her so strangely the words faded.

'I rely on the ethereal guidance of Al Hilal,' he said, and walked away; he was obviously a bit potty.

142

Harold didn't get to his feet for another two hours, by which time both Silver and Fury had lapsed into a tipsy sleep. He penned them a note thanking them for their hospitality, to which Rose added her name and a row of kisses.

CHAPTER FIFTEEN

Leaving Santa Ana, Harold fretted over his inability to express himself. He hadn't shone in the company of Fury and Silver. When discussing the killing of Dr King, they'd ignored his opinion, spoke over him, which was odd seeing that in his head he'd witnessed the blood spilling onto the floor. But then, with the exception of Shaefer, he'd often been thrust aside. Complaining to his mother all those lost years ago, her hair immaculately waved, eyes scornful, she'd said it was because he wasn't in command of his vocabulary. She was wrong because at college, sponsored by Shaefer, he'd once been up for president of the debating society.

Knowing that Wheeler would no longer be in Malibu, Harold quit the freeway and took the Pacific Coast Highway to Santa Monica. He kept the radio switched on to discourage Rose from chatting, without success. He had never met anyone so indifferent to nature. Blind to the pale blossoms of the paradise trees, the sugar-white sands edging the glitter of ocean, she fiddled with her top lip, her hair, the contents of her pockets, and gibbered mindlessly on about some medicine that had been used to combat foul language in Vietnam. She meant drugs, of course, in particular the lysergic acid which had affected the Philopsona woman.

He was annoyed with himself for having talked so freely to Fury. God knows why he'd spilled the beans about feelings for his mother, though he supposed the knitted rabbit on the chair had something to do with it. That and the drink. He'd droned on about his life before the arrival of a succession of stepfathers, the time when just the two of them had lived in a rundown apartment in Detroit, of the day when he was seven years old and she'd slapped his face because he'd left the soap in the washroom—it was communal, which accounted for his adult sensitivity to smells—and she'd feared it might get stolen. When he'd started to snivel she'd turned back and taken him in her arms. He remembered that hug because, ever after involved with men, it was the last time she'd shown him any affection. The telling of such childhood memories was embarrassing enough, but he feared he might also have gone on about Wheeler, perhaps even hinted at what he intended to do once they met.

Preoccupied, he narrowly avoided scraping the open door of a white Chevrolet, abandoned at the side of the road. Moments later he braked and got out, muttering to Rose that he needed to stretch his legs. Absorbed in the contents of her pockets, she just nodded. Stupidly, he left his hat behind and the sun was cruel on his head.

To the left of the camper, a slope led down to a small wood and as he made for its blue shadows he heard himself moan aloud. If he'd drunkenly confided in Fury and Silver, spat out his intentions, then surely they'd tell someone? He wasn't afraid of being found out, as long as he was successful. Was it possible they'd told Rose? When he'd woken

144

from sleep he'd heard Silver talking about violence and suffering, and she, eyes wide, had repeated the words.

He was loitering there, fingers tugging at his beard, when he heard the distinct and anguished noise of someone fighting for a last breath. He knew it was that because he'd been present when Frederick Beckstein had gurgled into death. The name had remained in his mind because it belonged to his third stepfather, the one who had taught him the value of investments and left him money in his will. Without Beckstein he might have been shoved into the boredom of earning a living.

Turning, he followed the direction of the sound and almost stumbled over a sprawled figure, hands pressed to a fragment of green cloth sticking to bloodstained white trousers. The face was as pale as the silver bead clipped to its earlobe. Harold stood there until the gasping stopped, then, waiting until his own breath slowed, knelt and placed a finger against the side of the man's throat. There was no pulse. In standing up his left knee accidentally slid across the white trousers, pinkly smearing his shorts. Near his feet the blade of a kitchen knife flashed sunlight. Frowning, he kicked it into the undergrowth and returned to the camper. A woman was sitting beside Rose, hands clasped as though in prayer.

'She was hitch-hiking,' Rose told him, 'and the man who picked her up attacked her, so she hit him and ran away. I said we'd give her a lift. We will, won't we?'

He nodded, there being nothing else he could do. When he took the wheel the woman slumped against him, the skirt of her green dress brushing

145

his leg. He drove off so quickly that she jerked forward, lank black hair spilling over her knees.

According to Rose, she was going to visit her brother in Newport, nine miles away. She had two brothers, the eldest of whom was away soldiering in Vietnam. The one she wanted to see—she needed to borrow money—had been born with a leg missing, which was why he was still at home. No, she didn't want to tell either him or the cops what had happened because then there'd be questions and she'd have to relive the horror. Besides, the brother with one leg was one of those ignorants who held that it was females who were to blame for sexual aggression, that men merely responded to signals. Rose agreed that not telling was sensible and said that once, when a man had pushed her down some stairs because she wouldn't have sex, she hadn't told anyone either. She'd injured her knee, not badly, just limped for a few days, but on account of her childhood she'd learned never to show hurt and that when in pain it was best to smile, seeing as an emotional reaction could often provoke another attack.

Appalled, Harold switched on the radio to shut her up, and above a Deanna Durbin love song heard an excited voice bursting out with the news that some woman had shot Andy Warhol, three times. Rose, tone truculent, asked him why Yanks kept shooting each other; was it because they were all allowed to own guns? It was obvious she'd never heard of Warhol.

Newport rose above the sandy shores of the Pacific, its main boulevard lined with palm trees. Ten years before, he and Dollie had come here to see a business acquaintance of hers supposedly

146

recovering from a heart attack, a journey that turned out to be wasted, seeing the guy was dead by the time they arrived. Dollie hadn't cried, simply got drunk, which was OK by him, though she didn't bother to shower as it made her want sex.

He asked the woman in the green dress where he should go, but she ignored him and began whispering to Rose, who presently directed him to a street with a hash house on the corner, its glass front steaming smoke yellow in the heat. A man wearing a sombrero stood outside, staring at a child who was kicking a yelping dog tied to a traffic pole.

Rose helped the woman out, and embraced her. Deanna Durbin had begun singing again and he slouched there, watching as Rose smoothed down the woman's hair, exposing a blob of blood, either her own or that of the man she had just stabbed, stuck to her cheek. He felt neither curious nor judgemental, seeing as he himself was heading towards the ultimate sin. Rose was now confronting the kid with the dog, untying its leash from the pole before she returned to the camper. The animal didn't run off, just sat there.

The woman waved and mouthed gratitude as she climbed the steps of her brother's house, but he knew she only saw Rose; he had become invisible, lost to all. As he reached the end of the street he looked into the side mirror and caught sight of the woman, now back on the sidewalk, scurrying in the opposite direction.

'It was a woman who shot Mussolini,' announced Rose, immersed as always in her own fantasies, 'though she didn't kill him.'

Her return plane ticket was in his wallet. He must remember to give it her before they reached

147

the hotel. She mustn't be with him when he encountered Wheeler . . . he had to be alone when the man who had ruined his life turned to face him, cold eyes flashing recognition . . .

Telling her he needed a drink, he drove until he came to a sign advertising beer. Sitting at the bar and observing her reflection in the mirror, eyes puffy, mouth tight, he said, 'Sorry to be irritable. I guess I'm tired.'

'It's normal,' she replied, 'for people who come from different backgrounds to find it difficult to get on. It's because we're programmed by the people who brought us up.'

It was disconcerting the way she often came out with an intelligent observation, and irritating when, as always, she quickly ruined it, suggesting that if they were squirrels, the very first ones without parents, knowing how to find nuts would be a matter of luck, not inheritance. 'If we didn't see our mothers scrabbling beneath a pine tree, how would we know what to do?' she enquired absurdly.

He ordered a large gin and concentrated on how to lose her when the opportunity came. As Wheeler was the only reason they were together she would obviously kick up a fuss if he stopped her accompanying him to the Ambassador Hotel. Worse, if she was in one of those moods which enabled her to see things clearly, she might interfere with his plans. They'd be in Los Angeles in two days' time and it sure would be easier if she got into the habit of going places on her own.

He said, 'I guess I've kept you on a leash, haven't I? I've been a shade controlling.'

She said, 'A shade, yes.'

'Well,' he said, 'there's a rather interesting

museum not far from here. You could go there on your own, if you want.'

She frowned at the word museum, until he explained that it wasn't the usual sort, that it had a large section on the lives of authors and painters.

'Which authors?' she asked.

'Robert Louis Stevenson, Upton Sinclair, John Steinbeck, Raymond Chandler . . .'

'Steinbeck,' she cried, 'I like him . . . I've read *Tortilla Flat*. What did the Chandler man write?'

'Crime novels,' he told her. 'He turned to writing when booze got him sacked from his job as an oil executive.'

'Drink,' she said, 'is a necessity for people who write. It makes the words come.' She then launched into a story about a woman she'd known who had always drunk whisky before writing short stories, but as she'd never got them published she'd turned to stealing library books, hundreds of them, which she sold to secondhand bookshops. It was very profitable and gave her a good life.

'I guess she ended up in jail,' he ventured.

'No,' she said. 'She ended up in a mansion in Somerset.'

After a second gin he escorted her round the block and gave her instructions on how to find the museum. She needn't hurry as he had some phone calls to make. He'd be in the bar in roughly an hour.

'Goody, goody,' she said, and ran off.

Returning to the camper, he wrote a letter to Shaefer expressing gratitude for his friendship and enclosing the address of the lawyer in charge of his will. Reading it over he tore it into pieces and penned another that didn't mention money.

Then he began scribbling a note to Polly and Bernard to thank them for introducing him to Rose, but he abandoned it halfway through the first sentence, irritation at the mere inking of her name drying up the words. And fond though he was of her, he didn't think it would be a good idea to write to Mirabella—plunged into depression, she'd wish him in hell for being the cause.

There being nobody else in his life who warranted either a goodbye or gratitude, he pocketed the pen and began to fold up the newspapers strewn across Rose's seat, at which he uncovered a bag with a broken zip. Stuffed inside was a grey jersey, a spotted dress, a pair of soiled panties and a purse containing two English pound notes and four dollars. Beneath was a lipstick, a toothbrush still in its wrapping, and a pocket diary without entries until the middle of May, and then each page blank but for the word 'Soon' written with a capital S. Blank that is, save for one line on March the twenty-eighth, 'Washington Harold is a very kind man,' and 'God how much longer,' on the thirtieth. As he dumped the bag under the seat, a cigarette lighter fell to the floor. It was made of silver and engraved with the initials JF.

He felt he deserved another drink. As he pushed open the camper door a blast of hot air took away his breath. Above him, a sweep of black cloud swallowed the blue of the sky. By the time he had a glass in his hand the world had turned dark and thunder cracked overhead.

The rain being heavy he expected Rose to be delayed, even though she permanently wore that crumpled raincoat. Then, as the downpour ceased and a further hour went by, he became uneasy. It was now eight o'clock and the museum was most likely shut. Hurrying along the damp sidewalk he began to cough from an inhalation of smoke, and on the next block encountered a noisy crowd halted by a line of policemen erecting barriers. The distant heavens were still dark, but now streaked with orange flame. A man tugged at his arm, looked into his face, asked if he knew what was burning, and for a moment he felt a surge of exhilaration at being noticed. Then an image of Rose, mouth open in a scream, shocked him into trembling reality.

CHAPTER SIXTEEN

It was so nice to be away from Harold that Rose couldn't stop smiling. She felt a touch bad about it seeing he'd been so good to her, driving her across the wilds of America, providing food and all that, but she couldn't help it. In a sense, she was doing him a favour—he was only being so obliging because he was lonely and needed someone to fill his life. She'd thought that without Harold at her side, Dr Wheeler would start coming back to her, but he didn't, no matter how hard she concentrated. It might have something to do with her being out of cigarettes. Walking beneath the dripping trees, she searched for a tobacco store.

She was standing outside a bar, digging into her pockets, when she realised she'd left her purse behind. She couldn't go back for it in case Harold underwent a change of heart and wouldn't allow her out of his sight again. Dismayed, she threaded her way between the umbrella-covered pedestrians, wondering whether she dared shoplift. Twice last year, caught redhanded, she'd struck the assistants as so childlike, so full of remorse, that they'd let her off, and on a third occasion, spinning a sad story about a cancer-stricken father desperate for a last smoke, the man behind the counter had given her a packet for nothing. But that was in England and attitudes were different in the States.

She was staring into the crowded interior of a café, rain flattening her hair, when she saw a man in a sports shirt striking a match. All the other tables were occupied, but he was alone, facing two empty seats. Remembering what she'd seen Mother do in Marshall's tea rooms in Southport, she entered and stood beside him, apparently intent on studying the menu chalked up on the wall behind the counter. She'd been assured that such an approach never failed, as long as the right bloke was chosen—but then Mother had only been pining for conversation.

Turning, she bumped against the man's chair and, exaggerating her English accent, apologised profusely. It worked and she was invited to sit down. In spite of her drowned appearance she could tell she excited him; being old and hairy, he was obviously used to women giving him the cold shoulder. He asked if he could buy her a drink and she said yes, a whisky, just a small one. Then he offered her a smoke. Rose confessed she wasn't all that keen on the habit, but she'd have one to keep him company. He had a large medal dangling from a chain round his neck, but as he was constantly fingering it she couldn't see what it represented.

The man's name was Walter Fedler and he owned racehorses. He seemed to be made of hair. It waved over his head, growing down to the tips of his ears; eyebrows, lashes, cheekbones, everything was dark and quivering with black wisps. He was here to meet a guy who wanted to buy a two-year-old mare. He himself hadn't got one at the moment, but he knew where he could find one. He'd met this guy by accident in Los Angeles last week, when his truck was waiting at the lights on Wilshire Boulevard. He was on the sidewalk talking to an older man, and as the lights began to change he held up a hand and asked if he could hitch a ride to the Plaza Hotel.

'We talked about him being a jockey and having been born in Jordan, which was kind of coincidental seeing me and the wife are planning a holiday in Jerusalem. When he said he wanted to buy a mare I told him I could find him one for maybe three hundred and fifty dollars and he said three hundred was his limit.'

'This is awfully interesting,' Rose said, 'though for some reason it's making me want to smoke.' He handed her another one instantly.

Pleased at her involvement, Mr Fedler continued his monologue. He knew all about horses because he'd worked as a stablehand as a boy. Then he'd drummed with the Tommy Dorsey Band, only he'd had to pack it in owing to his wrists swelling up from all that thumping.

After that he'd got a job in a Pasadena bookstore specialising in occult subjects, which had led to him acquiring hyno-programming skills and treating shell-shocked veterans of the Korean War. Now he was on the board of the American Institute of Hypnosis. It was an important position.

He was still involved in medical practice, instructing others. Hypnosis required concentration,

153

self-belief. The guy he was waiting for could be put under almost instantly. 'Tell Sirhan to do something, no matter what,' he said, 'and he'll do it.'

'Blimey,' said Rose.

'I bet,' he confided, leaning close and breathing into her face, 'I could hypnotise everyone in this place in less than five minutes.'

Gazing into his bloodshot eyes she was tempted to tell him to go ahead, but at that moment the man he was expecting arrived. It was yellow sweater, only he was wearing a black leather jacket.

Although he neither looked at Rose nor addressed her directly, she knew he recognised her. He was, she reasoned, immensely shy of women on account of being from Arabia. Arabic men were taught that women were inferior and only important on account of sex, and being religious they had to avoid contamination. Not that he talked much to Fedler either, merely nodded a lot as the old man rambled on about the condition of the mare and what it was worth. When Fedler left to go to the toilet, yellow sweater began drumming his fingers on the table.

'It was kind of you to give me a cigarette the other day,' Rose said, hoping he'd offer her another one. He didn't, nor did he reply, just went on tapping in that agitated way he had. She smiled at him, but he was leaning back in his chair, staring up at the ceiling. The silence continued; she fidgeted, searching for something to say. Suddenly he sat up straight, moistened his lips and asked, 'You have been here before?'

'No,' she said. 'Not here I haven't.'

'You have much money?'

'No,' she said. 'Hardly any.'

'You are content with your holiday?'

'It's not a holiday,' she corrected. 'I'm searching for someone.'

'They owe you money?'

'No,' she said, 'he's not like that.'

'They have seen much of you?' he persisted.

She said, 'Not for years, but it doesn't matter because he understands me.' She would have elaborated further if Fedler hadn't returned.

The two men left almost immediately, Fedler being in a hurry to show yellow sweater the mare. Rose thought of following them, but changed her mind. It would look as if she was desperate for company, which she wasn't. What she needed was somewhere quiet, a place where she could concentrate on what was going to happen when she was reunited with Dr Wheeler. She asked the waitress if there was a church nearby and was told to turn left past a white truck parked down the street.

The church was small, huddled between a funeral parlour and a furniture showroom. Above the door hung a plaster statue of Our Lord, the toes of his left foot broken off, holding up his hand in a gesture of blessing. It was a pity there wasn't a graveyard outside, like the one she and Dr Wheeler had strolled through all those years ago. In the presence of the dead, he'd said, one was more conscious of being alive.

The inside of the church was empty, save for a man on his knees and a woman with a beehive hairstyle lighting a candle beneath an image of the Virgin Mary. The praying man had a bad cough. Rose had once been picked up in a church. When

155

she'd told Dr Wheeler about it he'd laughed and said the man must have thought his prayers had been answered.

Rose didn't kneel, just slouched, gazing at the altar. Thoughts and questions tumbled through her head. If, when she got back, Polly and Bernard asked for her impressions of America she wouldn't find it easy, the miles having cascaded past in a swirl of sun-scorched days. She supposed she might waft on about Mr Nixon and how unfair it was that Mr Kennedy, the JFK one, had cheated him out of the presidency because he was so rich, but she wasn't sure she'd get the facts right. She could come up with a few place names . . . Chicago, Yellowstone Park, Wanakena . . . and that town where Harold had wet himself in the bank, but not much else. No point mentioning the gun held to her head, they'd only accuse her of lying, like the time she'd told them about Father hanging her out of the window because she'd called him a bugger. What would happen when she got to Los Angeles . . . how would Dr Wheeler react? What if he suggested she should stay and get a job, or even work for him, offered to fix her up in a nice flat, one with its own bathroom? Of course she wouldn't let him pay for it, that would be wrong, even though he could afford it. With her English accent she could find employment in a bookshop . . . she'd be good at that. She wasn't sure what work Dr Wheeler did, but she could be a sort of hostess when he gave a dinner party . . . or just someone who opened the door and took coats and hats . . . she'd need another dress . . . and proper shoes, scarlet ones with high heels . . . She'd jump at the chance of staying, there being nothing much to go back for, no one she really cared

156

about—apart from Bernard's boxer dog—no future that really mattered . . .

The praying man stood up and made for the door. She followed him because he was digging into his pocket and she thought he might be reaching for a cigarette, but the beehive woman barred her way, clutching her arm and asking if she knew where the priests lived. Her husband had left her, she wailed, and she'd just found out she was pregnant; she needed money.

'Wait here,' Rose said, 'my father will have some.'

By the time she stepped outside the man had disappeared. She walked back to where she had left Harold. He wasn't in the bar, nor the van. She sat on the running board and waited. A quarter of an hour went by until she spied him at the top of the street. When he saw her he broke into a run. She prepared herself for a ticking off for being away too long, but when he drew level he pulled her upright and hugged her fiercely. She could feel his beard tickling her neck. When he let go and stood back she noticed his eyes were watering. Surprised, she asked him what was wrong.

'The museum's on fire. I was afraid you were inside.'

'I never got to the museum,' she said. 'I got involved with a pregnant woman.'

He seemed in such a good mood that when they got into the van she was daring enough to light a cigarette. Again, he surprised her by saying how much he liked the smell of tobacco, on account of it bringing back happy memories of college days with Shaefer. She was warming to him when, about to start the engine, he said, 'I need to give you your plane ticket, in case we lose each other, and money for a cab. I guess it'll be pretty crowded in the hotel with Kennedy in town. We might get separated.'

'I'm not sure I'll need it,' she told him. 'Dr Wheeler may ask me to stay on.'

'Take it,' he ordered, face tightening. 'One never knows what could happen. There might be a disturbance.'

'Disturbance?' she echoed.

'The Republicans will be there in force. There could be a full-scale riot.'

He plonked the ticket and some dollars into her lap. As she attempted to stuff them into her pocket he seized her arm and demanded she put them somewhere safe. His tone was so authoritative that she ferreted under the seat for her bag and did as she was told. Inwardly she cursed him for being so bossy.

'That zip doesn't work,' he snapped, taking a length of string from the shelf beneath the dashboard. 'Use this to tie up the top.'

She felt there was something bothering him, bigger than the possible loss of a ticket. Several times on the journey he'd complained of a dicky tummy; maybe it was playing up again. Even so, he had no right to treat her like a child. She slumped back and fiddled with the piece of string. As he drove off she pushed the bag under her feet, then, greatly daring, asked him how long it would take them to reach Malibu. He said they weren't going to Malibu, not tonight. He was too tired, and in any case he needed to go to Santa Monica. He had something important to do.

'But you promised.'

'I'd have gone there yesterday,' he told her, 'if

158

you hadn't got us mixed up with that woman who'd had a fight in the woods.'

They drove through a mist, salt-laden, borne upwards from the sea, and suddenly he asked if she'd been telling the truth when she'd said Dr Wheeler had a wife. It was an unexpected question. Again she described the woman on the bicycle she'd seen when visiting the chip shop as a child.

'I've heard all that,' he interrupted. 'I want to know how old she was, what nationality . . . did you ever hear her called Mrs Wheeler?'

'Lots of times. The man in the chippie knew her, and so did my dad.'

'But it could have been his sister,' he argued, 'she could have been a Miss not Mrs.'

So she told him about the time she'd spied on Dr Wheeler through the lounge window of his house and how she'd seen the two of them writhing about on the couch, she with her knickers around her ankles and he with his bottom in the air. That shut him up. She didn't tell him that she'd stayed there, watching as Dr Wheeler poured himself a drink, watching as his wife, skirt pulled down, sat on the couch with a magazine on her lap, lips moving as she read, sandalled feet planted firmly on the carpet. There'd been no change in the woman's sensible face, no transfiguration of joy or bliss, and the eyes Dr Wheeler turned to the window were empty and dry.

They parked in an area of ground above a beach. As it was dark she could see nothing beyond a chain of bobbing lights, which she reasoned must belong to fishing boats anchored in the bay. When she licked her lips she tasted the sea. She wanted to ask if they were still in Newport, but he looked so

159

severe she didn't dare.

It was a posh campsite, each plot separated from the next by a row of trees, and each illuminated by a lamp on a pole. Nearby was a wooden gate leading to a provision shop and a row of washrooms. She'd reckoned Harold would want to start cooking right away, seeing as they hadn't eaten since Mrs Fury's chicken; instead he muttered that he wasn't hungry and was going straight to bed. She supposed she'd been right about his stomach. For once he didn't change into his dressing gown and march off with towel and toilet bag, just tossed his shoes out of the van and half closed the doors. She could hear him talking to himself. Walking away, she listened to the sounds filling the shadows, a tinkle of radio music, the smack of an axe chopping wood, the hum of the sea as it danced across the sands.

Somewhere out in the black night Dr Wheeler stood waiting for her, trilby hat raised in greeting.

*   *   *

In sleep, Rose flung out an arm across Harold's throat, jolting him awake some time before dawn. He crawled from the camper and walked barefoot towards a stretch of grass beyond the provision store. He would have roamed about if he hadn't encountered two men sitting in deckchairs, smoking cigars. They nodded at him, but he walked on into the half light, his mind a confused mixture of resolution and indecision. It was, he realised, imperative he leave Newport as quickly as possible. It could be that his facial expression, the quiver of his hand when signing the receipt, had been noted and that already he was under scrutiny. As he

160

hurried back to the camper, he was convinced that the deckchair men eyed him with more than casual interest. The sooner he got rid of his beard the better.

Returning, he found Rose up and packing her belongings. She told him she'd been disturbed in the night by the scurrying of rats. He didn't tell her she was mistaken, that what she'd heard were raccoons. Conscious he'd been rough with her the day before, he made an effort to be civil, until, emptying the rubbish and spying his shorts in the wastebin, she questioned him about his health. She seemed to think he had a problem with his stomach. She wasn't prying, she said, just concerned for his well-being. Incensed by her interest in his bowels, he reminded her about the woman in the woods. 'Unlike you,' he snarled, 'I dislike contamination.'

They left at first light, driving towards Santa Monica so fast that they twice skidded when rounding a bend. Both times Rose was jolted against the dashboard; she didn't cry out, merely scrabbled at her lip, a habit which infuriated him. He was so edgy it was a struggle not to smack her hand away from her mouth.

Anxious to seem normal he began to whistle. Then, aware she was staring at him, he drew her attention to a flowering weed in the hedgerow. She paid no heed, remaining sprawled in her seat. It was only when he pointed at the distant sun-blurred spread of Malibu that she sat up and stared out of the window.

Santa Monica was perched on yellow bluffs bordering Palisades Park, a narrow strip of land studded with towering palm trees and tropical plants. On Third Street Promenade he found

161

the place he was searching for and slammed on the brakes. Ordering Rose to stay put, he hurried inside.

He was in the chair, a towel about his neck, when a picture came to him of his mother, one eye shut, mouth open, plucking her eyebrows. She'd always done it at the kitchen table without bothering to remove the cloth, and when she put food in front of him hairs drifted along the rim of his plate. He saw the clippings so clearly that he shook his head to be rid of the image, and felt the sharp edge of the razor scrape across his skin.

A tuft of cotton wool stuck to the cut on his cheek, he clambered back into the camper and waited for Rose to comment on his changed appearance. She didn't. She just sat there, head down, pretending to study the road map.

Looking at her, clothes shabby, hair dishevelled, he decided she had to clean herself up. If she didn't and was still at his side in Los Angeles, he doubted they'd let him into the hotel. As soon as he started the engine she asked if they were at last going to Malibu.

'Not yet,' he told her.

'Why not?'

'We both need a bath, you in particular.'

'Americans are funny,' she said, 'always going on about washing. I expect it's because you've always been used to constant hot water.'

He paid for a room in a motel within walking distance of Palisades Park. The room didn't have a bathtub, just a shower. Glaring at him as if he'd deliberately planned to upset her, she ordered him to wait outside. He heard the water running, though only for a minute or so, and then she shouted that she was done. When he went back inside, she was already in her clothes, and as she bent to pull on her shoes he noticed her feet were still grubby. She swore she'd washed her hair, though when they returned to the camper the shampoo bottle was poking out of her bag, unopened.

Before setting off for Malibu he rang John Fury at the office in Los Angeles to make sure he'd be at the Ambassador Hotel on the fifth. Fury said the date was underscored in his diary, then relayed some gossip about the Kennedy campaign. Apparently Kennedy was so popular with the crowds they repeatedly ripped off his cufflinks, even tore away his shirt sleeves. 'But he's in real danger,' Fury said, 'and he knows it. A week ago, staying in Frankenheimer's beach house, someone asked him if he realised he was likely to be killed. "It's a chance I have to take," he replied. "How many attempts were there on de Gaulle's life . . . six, seven? I guess we'll just have to put our hope in that old bitch, luck."'

'Hope my ass,' said Harold as he put down the phone. He didn't give a shit about Kennedy, only that Fury would secure him entrance to the hotel.

The Pacific Coast Highway was drenched in sunlight, the sea below rippling silver as it stroked the beach. Rose, now that she believed they were about to find Wheeler, became animated. Harold's generosity, she gushed, his selflessness, was overwhelming. Lots of people in her life had been kind to her, but none as kind as he. 'You,' she vowed, 'will be remembered in my prayers,' which made him grimace.

Half an hour later he brought the camper to a halt at the lower end of the Malibu Beach road, and

163

explained they couldn't go further as everything ahead was privately owned. Rose, shielding her eyes from the dazzling whiteness of the detached houses fronting the ocean, wanted to know in which one they'd find Dr Wheeler. He admitted he wasn't sure.

'The people here must have money coming out of their ears,' she commented.

'Bing Crosby has a place here,' he said, 'and Cary Grant. It's not open to the public. I'll have to make a telephone call to gain admission.'

There was a parking lot at the back of a provision store with a children's roundabout flashing sunlight as it whirled in a circle. Rose stayed put, which suited him. He bought a candy bar and kept an eye on the camper, in case Rose came in search of him. When he returned with the news that Wheeler had again moved on, she looked as if she would burst into tears. He assured her they'd definitely find him in Los Angeles tomorrow, at the Ambassador Hotel.

She didn't want to go for a swim; he had to force her out onto the beach. When he waded into the sea, he was conscious of her slumped on the sands behind him, a hand shielding her eyes. As usual she'd forgotten to bring her sunglasses.

Floating on his back, eyes shut against the sun, he was blinded by an image in his head of that refined face, mouth curved in a superior smile. He tried to empty his mind of Wheeler, without success.

CHAPTER SEVENTEEN

'Sit up straight,' Washington Harold said. Leaning forward he slapped Rose's hand away from her mouth. He had reassured her often enough that there was nothing wrong with her lip, that it was all in her imagination. Rose blinked, then turned her head away and appeared to study the occupants of the Colonial Room. Her gaze was fixed on the young man with the funny name who, scratching the shoulder of his yellow sweater, was scribbling words into an exercise book with a red cover. From the Embassy Ballroom beyond came the plucking notes of banjos and voices raucously singing.

'I'm sorry,' Harold said. 'I didn't mean to slap you.'

'That wasn't a slap,' she replied. 'It was a blow.'

He remained silent for some minutes, gliding the tip of his forefinger round and round the rim of his wineglass. At last, he repeated, 'I'm sorry. I guess all that driving has worn me down.'

'I won't be a moment,' Rose said, and left the table. At the door she paused, tilting her head to catch the dying whine of the singing glass.

The lobby of the Ambassador Hotel was panelled in dark wood set with mirrors. The lamps were lit and whichever way she turned she caught her reflection fleeing across glass. The dazzle obscured the crumpled state of her polka-dot dress.

Yesterday, Washington Harold had booked them into a motel in Santa Monica to have a bath, only there wasn't one, just a shower. She couldn't abide showers; the water was either scalding or icy and

165

standing up was a daft way to get washed. When he saw her emerge he'd said it was odd that her hair wasn't wet and she'd said it dried very quickly. She knew he knew she was lying, but no longer cared. It wasn't her fault they came from different backgrounds.

There was an iron in the room and if Harold hadn't been so impatient to get to his breakfast she might have attended to her dress. He'd ordered three eggs, a double portion of ham and a mound of fried potatoes. He cut up the ham and then did away with the knife and speared everything with a fork, the way children did. Although she was hungry she only asked for two slices of toast; she was determined not to cause him further expense.

After breakfast they'd got into the camper again and drove to Malibu. It was the place where John Fury had last seen Dr Wheeler. It was windy and the waves bounced towards the clouds. Harold changed into bathing trunks and trotted down to the gusty sea on tiptoe like a bandy ballet dancer. From a distance he looked less podgy, more in proportion with the sky. He hadn't asked her if she would join him; by now he knew what her answer would be.

The beach was deserted save for some children and three men, one of whom wore bathing shorts and proceeded to chase the shrieking youngsters across the sand; leapfrogging into the furled waves, they dipped and rose like skimmed pebbles. Dressed in city suits, the two onlookers paced up and down, passing each other, sentry fashion.

Rose watched them rather than Harold; deep down she wished him drowned. Suddenly a wave spiralled up, submerging one of the children, at which the suited men ran forward waving their arms and hollering. The buoyant adult plunged downward and scooped up the endangered water-baby in one fist. Tossed on shore, the small figure was engulfed in a towel and slapped vigorously on the back. It wasn't cuddled.

When Rose, voice quivering, told Washington Harold what she'd seen, he said it didn't do to focus on what might have happened, better to rejoice at a fortunate result. Most deaths, he opined, were accidental, even the vicious ones. He'd then spent some minutes, all the time energetically towelling himself, relating the fate of a child in Chicago who was in the habit of ringing doorbells and then running away. Mrs Fantano, a widow, had been subjected daily to this annoyance by a nine-year-old girl living in the apartment above. One teatime Mrs Fantano had lain in wait, and, opening the door the instant the buzzing sizzled the air, had seized the delinquent by the hair, at which the child turned blue in the face and expired. Terrified, Mrs Fantano had inserted a broom handle into the girl's anus and dragged the body onto the fire-escape. She hadn't known the offender had a weak heart.

Rose would have liked to ask questions, but the word anus put her off. It was just like Harold not to refer to that part as a bottom.

She was thinking about words while standing in the lobby of the hotel, in particular 'Cocoanut Grove', the name of the famous nightclub she'd been told had real palm trees growing between the tables and stuffed monkeys hanging from the branches. The interior had been used by James Cagney in the film *Lady Killer*. 'I hate him,' she said out loud, but she was thinking of Harold; she liked Cagney, even though he was undersized and frowned a lot.

She asked a bellboy to show her the entrance to the club. There was a stout man shouting into a walkie-talkie outside the glass doors. 'Please,' Rose said, 'I want to see the ceiling embedded with stars.'

He said, 'Come again?'

'I'm from England,' she elaborated. 'I've just come to peep at the monkeys.'

'No can do,' he said, and turned his back on her.

She retreated into the nearby powder room and attempted to comb her hair. The sea air that morning had made it sticky. She was tugging away when two women entered; one wore a cheeky boater encircled with a band of stars and stripes, the other clutched a bald baby. Posturing at the mirror, a licked finger moistening an eyebrow, the boater woman said, 'I guess he's home and dry, Connie,' to which the other retorted, 'It don't do to get too confident. Time sure has a way of altering things.' Wide-eyed, the baby stared at Rose, waiting for a smile of love. She turned away.

When the women had gone she looked at her face in the mirror, at the tear balanced on her cheek. I won't always be unhappy, she reassured herself, and flicked it into the basin. Soon Dr Wheeler would take care of her, and then everything would be different.

Washington Harold was no longer at the table when she returned to the Colonial Room. He was standing in a crowd of people massed outside the propped-open doors of the ballroom. Above the noise of the banjos, voices were screaming, 'We want Bobby . . .' followed by tumultuous applause and the deafening shrill of whistles.

John Fury joined her. He looked buoyant. 'He's in,' he said. 'Time for a new America.'

Fury was a good man; it was he who had located Dr Wheeler and confirmed that he was part of the Kennedy entourage. He'd even discovered that Wheeler had spent the previous night in the house of a film man called Frankenheimer, who was entertaining Robert Kennedy to dinner.

The man in the yellow sweater had leapt onto a chair, the better to see over the heads at the door. Rose took her shoes off and did the same, and watched as a youngish man with floppy hair mounted the steps onto the stage. He patted the air with his hand in an attempt to quell the noise and spoke into the microphone, to little effect. The crowd screamed even louder. 'You can't hear,' he shouted. 'Can we get something that works . . . Can we . . .' Now his voice became stronger, though he had to bellow to be heard above the continuing uproar. Often his words were lost.

'What I think is . . . what I think is quite clear is that we can work together in the last analysis . . . the violence, the disenchantment with our society . . . the division, whether between black and white, between the poor and the . . . over the war in Vietnam . . . We are a great country, a compassionate . . . and I intend to make that my basis . . . we can start to work together.'

Harold moved away from the door and gestured to her to get off the chair. She hadn't the confidence to defy him. He held out a hand to help her, but she wouldn't give him the satisfaction. Without his beard he lacked authority. Abruptly, he told her to stay where she was and not to follow him. He had something important to do;

169

he wouldn't be long. Then he leaned close to John Fury and whispered something in his ear.

She sat very still and watched him go. He turned back and clumsily patted her shoulder. He said, 'You look really great in that dress. Did I tell you that?'

'No,' she said, 'you didn't.'

'Really great,' he repeated, and then, fingers piercing her arm, hissed, 'I'm only doing what's best. We're all looking for something.' Then he walked in the direction of the service doors to the left of the ballroom.

'Or someone,' she murmured. A star of blood, delicate as a snowflake, melted upon her upper lip.

Beryl Bainbridge was in the process of finishing *The Girl in the Polka-dot Dress* when she died on 2 July 2010. Her long-time friend and editor, Brendan King, prepared the text for publication from her working manuscript, taking into account suggestions Beryl made at the end of her life. No additional material has been included.